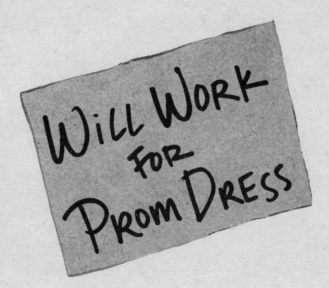

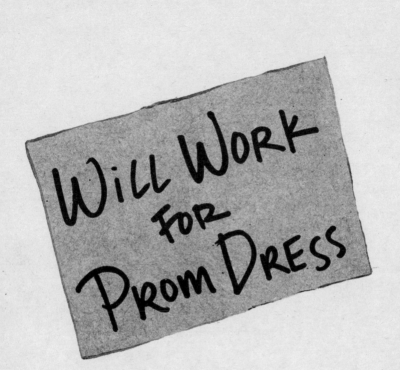

Aimee Ferris

SCHOLASTIC INC.
New York Toronto London Auckland
Sydney Mexico City New Delhi Hong Kong

ISBN 978-0-545-37468-2

12 11 10 9 8 7 6 5 4 3 2   11 12 13 14 15 16/0

Printed in the U.S.A.   40

First Scholastic printing, May 2011

Will work for Nakoa (happily)

• •

Chapter One

"Pepperoni, pepperoni. Cheese, cheese, cheese. Pepperoni, pepperoni. Cheese, cheese, chee—" I yelled.

"Quigley! Do you have to do that?" shouted Anne, my best friend and the person responsible for my current state of misery.

"Anne, I have been elbow deep in tomato sauce for six afternoons, now. I have to do something to break the monotony, or I'm going to knock old Helga aside and slit my wrists with her cheese grater!"

At some point during my tirade, the roar of the assembly-line machinery halted, letting my words sail through the warehouse. I couldn't be sure exactly when the noise stopped. Judging by the nasty look I was getting from the German-accented lady to my right, I had to assume it was before I called her "old." Or "Helga."

Anne and I had not made many friends here in the frozen-pizza factory. But that was not our goal. We came to make some cash and split as soon as our measly paychecks covered our dress tabs for formal. Four months to find financing and dates. It was a toss-up as to which was less likely to happen.

The assembly line cranked back up with a roar, and the doughy disks passed by in a blur.

"Quick!"

Anne squealed as three pizzas flew by her "untopped." I tossed what I could at them before we found our rhythm again and returned to our screaming chat.

"You could have at least found us a gig at a chocolate factory? Like that old TV clip they always show—the *I Love Lucy* one?"

"What?" yelled Anne.

"You know, that one where they're stuffing chocolates in their mouths, and down their tops, and everywhere else 'cause they can't keep up?"

"Chicken cutlets!"

"What?"

This was getting ridiculous, my voice was going to go any minute.

"I *said* chicken cutlets. The models, they use those things that look like chicken cutlets if they don't have real implants," she said.

"Have the garlic fumes gotten to you? What are you going on about?"

"You were talking about stuffing your top," Anne said. "I don't know why you're complaining anyway—if anyone needs it, I do. But the models use those silicone thingies they call chicken cutlets. I've never seen a raw chicken cutlet. I guess they look the same, or something?"

"No, no. It was this old TV show. Ah, just forget it."

I decided to save my voice and my sanity. Both were liable to leave me for good at any moment. What to do? Halfway done, two more hours to go. I decided to resume the little game I'd started four days earlier. The goal was to make a portrait on the pizza of the lady across the line from me using only my incredible, but as yet undiscovered, artistic talent. And some sausage.

The first day, the "portraits" looked pretty much like smiley clown faces. It all started with me trying to get a laugh out of Anne without the supervisor giving me "the look." But I was quite proud of some of my recent creations. The key was to get Anne to double her time and top most of the pizzas herself. That way I could work my magic on the moving line of blank canvas dough discs for a good twenty seconds before they were off to packaging, and then into the wild blue yonder. Or the steel-gray oven of some busy mom or frat house.

"Check it out!" I nudged Anne and pointed out my muse. Her giggles at my choice could almost be heard over the assembly line.

We all stood, covered in large white rubber aprons that reached our knees, with nasty damp gloves pulled up past our elbows. This ensemble—the latest in lunch-lady fashion—was topped with the classic, the ever-timeless accessory, the hairnet. Except ours looked like hotel shower caps.

Basically, everyone on the assembly line looked the same, give or take sixty pounds and sixty years. But my muse . . . well, she was just different. I don't think of myself as unkind, but this poor woman had a mole on the top of her nose that protruded so far I couldn't figure out how she didn't end up cross-eyed. Anne had a theory. The woman was also afflicted with floofy eyebrows that seemed to fly out at the sides instead of lying flat. Anne was betting, with her superior knowledge of ocular physics, that they might pull her vision focus out instead of dead center, thus compensating for the nose mole.

This was just the sort of challenge I needed to occupy the rest of my shift. This would take calculation. This would take expertise. This would take—an olive.

I took careful aim, with Anne poised, ready to assist.

"Go!"

Anne's hands worked at lightning speed as she squirted sauce and tossed handfuls of cheese and meat randomly across the coming pies. I waited for just the right moment, then lunged across her and whipped down a light base of cheese and created a quick jawline with the unnaturally round sausage pellets.

"Sauce me!"

Anne shoved the tube into my right hand like a well-trained surgical nurse. I swirled an outline to frame my portrait. Tearing a pepperoni slice in half, I made some mournful eyes. The woman's eyes were not really mournful, but, in my opinion, they should have been.

"Cheese!"

I grabbed great handfuls of mozzarella to create the perfect shower cap–hairnet effect, and *la pièce de résistance* (who said French class never taught you anything useful?)—the olive mole. This final touch I made while crashing into the sturdy heft of "Helga" before the pizza disappeared under its cloak of shrink-wrap. But the job was done. We'd come close before, but the olive really topped it.

Anne jumped up and down on her half of the little stepping stool we shared. We high-fived and screamed in victory until "the look" was given, and we bent our backs to our work once again.

On the way home, Anne and I jogged and chatted. Well, she jogged, and I cursed her back and wheezed as I tried to keep up. It was just my bad luck that I'd picked a friend who lived at the very top of College Hill. This was all part of Anne's little plan of improvement she'd decided we should undertake to achieve prom nirvana. We saved our bus money and got in shape for those perfect, slinky dresses, all at the same time.

Personally, I thought we should have been doing something to reward ourselves just for making it through the day. First, eight hours of school—well, seven and a half for Anne. She hooked up with her college-guy boyfriend at his place during the first half of trig. She had worked out that, by school rules, she could be up to thirty minutes late without a parent's note. Five "lates" got you one after-school detention. Five after-school detentions were worth one Saturday morning detention spent picking up trash in the football stadium.

It took five of those before the administration bothered to call a parent for one day of suspension.

Anne weighed the benefit/risk equation and chose her morning freedom, since her afternoons were monitored, minute by minute, by her mom. By her accounts, she had fourteen more mornings before the big call to Ms. Parisi. By *my* accounts, after doing all that math, Anne really wasn't missing much in trig.

"Wait up!" I put it into overdrive and closed the distance. Sweat stung my eyes, ruining the view of the stately, ivy-covered brick homes on Anne's steep, cobblestone street. We lived in different worlds, joined together, thankfully, by one arts-centered charter school.

Slipping back into history and imagining life spent in one of the expensive-looking houses was a good way to distract me from the burning sensation behind my right thigh. Inhaling the smell of fresh-cut heirloom roses from the garden, while sitting for portraits in the parlor or waiting for your horse-drawn carriage . . . well, that just had to beat sucking in the stench of Bengay, slathered on while yelling out *Wheel of Fortune* answers in the den of my beige, cookie-cutter, split-level ranch.

"What?" Anne interrupted my romantic musings.

"Just thinking. You can't be running around with Brad all morning anymore."

"It's Chad. And why not?"

Ah. Chad. They always started as some four-letter name and usually ended the same way. The ending names were a lot more colorful, though.

"Well, you can't be pulling afternoon detentions if we're going to make it to work on time."

"Oh, crap. You're right. Guess I'll have to save my last thirteen 'lates' till closer to the dance."

"I thought you had fourteen left."

"Fourteen and they call! Can't have that, can we? Hey, maybe it starts over with the spring semester!"

"Yeah, good luck with that."

"Jealous!"

"You wish."

"Let's sprint the last half mile. Race ya home!" And she was off.

"Wench!"

I huffed as I tried to pick up my knees to follow. At least working in the pizza factory had destroyed any love I once held for my former major food group. I couldn't even walk down the frozen-food aisle without gagging.

This was all so much more important to Anne. Her mother was Victoria Parisi, internationally acclaimed fashion designer, specializing in bridal gowns. She always offered to make Anne, and me—her unofficially adopted daughter—our dresses.

I was thrilled. Anne was not. This might have had something to do with our last three formals when Ms. Parisi claimed to be so busy that she had to finish Anne's dress the afternoon of the dance.

This, Anne could deal with. We had fabric swatches for buying our shoes and accessories ahead of time. But suspiciously, despite otherwise exemplary time-management skills, Anne's mom would always need to sew her into the dress at the last minute. Sewn in, meaning no one still could sample the goods.

"No time for a zipper! But no problem, dear, let me just whipstitch this back closed."

Ms. Parisi was not a stupid woman.

• • • • • • • • • • •

By the time I panted through the Parisis' front door, Anne was already sitting with her long, sweaty legs thrown across a velvet ottoman. With one hand she flipped through the channels. The other held a diet soda. A second can's sweat was sliding precariously down near the high-gloss wood of the coffee table where it sat, sans coaster. I snatched it up, wiped off the ring, and sat down gingerly on the antique sofa.

Anne laughed at my discomfort.

"It's a house, not a museum."

"But still—"

"Don't be so impressed. Mummy Dear will be replacing all this with the latest trend within the month."

"What're we watching?"

"News."

"No, really."

"Really," Anne said. "Didn't you read my e-mail outlining the Betterment Plan?"

"Betterment Plan? The Plan of Improvement has a new name?"

"Well, you wouldn't stop calling it POI, which gave me nightmares of my Maui trip and that gray Hawaiian pudding. I could barely down the *poi*, even though I was trying to impress those hot hula guys."

She shuddered. "According to the BP, learning about current events will help us attract men who are more mature and exciting. You don't want to be tied down to high school boys, do you?"

"I think I'll pass on being tied down to any sort of boy for the moment. Sounds more like your area."

She threw a small pillow at me, almost toppling a vase so ugly it must have been worth a fortune, which I quickly righted.

"Hardy har har, *Mom*. But really, let's improve ourselves, shall we?"

She settled on a tabloid-news station. I hid my smirk. After a brief look at the latest little celeb runt named after some piece of fruit or Druid season, a very strange image covered the screen.

"What *is* that?" Anne asked.

I scooted to the edge of the little couch for a better look.

"Looks almost like a piz—"

"Oh my—"

"Holy—"

"Turn it up, turn it up!" I yelled.

I sat, staring at the vision in mozzarella and saw Anne's dream of a zippered dress slowly melt away. A newswoman stood in front of a crowd of Elvis impersonators. A heavyset "older" Elvis spoke with passion into the big black microphone and shook the pizza at the camera. The extra cheese of the hairnet had melted up and browned into a very convincing pompadour the King himself would have been proud to sport.

"It's him. We've said for years he was still out there. He's giving us a sign he's alive! We've been laughed at—ridiculed—for believing. We told you, 'don't be cruel,' baby, but you were. It was 'heartbreak hotel' for us, but look at this! You can't deny it's him!"

The breathless man in the sparkly white jumpsuit was pushed aside by, well, another man in a sparkly white jumpsuit. In the background, women and men alike clung to each other and wept for joy through their mass rendition of "Blue Suede Shoes."

"We've seen it. And we're not the only ones! We have another bus on the way to Rockville where they've spotted two more. Look at his mournful eyes. 'Are you lonesome tonight,' Elvis?" the man pleaded into the camera before turning back to the newscaster. "You can see it—he's so lonesome he could weep. This is a cry of help from the King. And we *will* find him."

"Well, there you have it. Our investigative reporting team is on the trail of where these 'Elvi-pie' originated. We'll be back after these messages with footage from Rockville, where Elvis's faithful have set up a shrine in the great man's honor."

The report faded out as the crowd started the first bars of "Love Me Tender."

Anne clicked the TV off. We sat in stunned silence for three seconds before bursting into laughter.

"Helga will be so happy," Anne said.

"Yep. This will make her day. We better hit the help-wanted sites."

Chapter Two

• •

I sat in the cafeteria and doodled in my new, fabric-covered notebook. It was more of a journal than a proper school notebook. A little treat I gave myself after being unceremoniously fired from my first real job. The man actually used the words "possible criminal assault on an Italian food product."

I thought about correcting him and explaining that pizza originated in ancient Middle Eastern cultures. I might be a C+ student, but I was wise in the ways of pizza. But he was already sputtering and turning a disturbing shade of purple. It would be ironic for a man who made his living filling arteries with trans fats to keel over from a stress-related heart attack or stroke.

I actually felt a little bad for him. The man was still

getting death threats printed on fake memorabilia from the pseudo-Elvi. The throngs of faithful followers took offense, thinking the mess was some kind of publicity stunt exploiting their love for the King. Anne's suggestion that he give up the frozen-food business and open a Blue Suede Shoe Shop didn't go over very well.

My journal doodle morphed into a smiling pizza.

I had a weird fetish for brand-new stationery and school supplies. Sadly, I didn't find school nearly as thrilling as the smell of freshly lined loose leaf. Most days, I stared at the stains on the badly painted walls trying to find faces or animal shapes, like a depressing version of the old cloud game. I counted the minutes until art class, the sole education-related bright spot in my day.

Through much haggling and hard work to keep up my other regular classes, I had managed to eke out space for three art classes in each of my previous schedules. After such a lackluster response to my initial round of art institute applications, my parents decided I should concentrate on academics this semester to secure a spot at a regular college, majoring in the arts. So Print Photography it was, the only course not conflicting with one of the pillars of academia.

Technically, in the photography class, I held the "teacher's assistant" position—not a true student. I still managed to get my hands into one of my own projects now and then when I wasn't busy mixing outdated developing chemicals. But without my mental art breaks throughout the day, I felt like a little kid who'd had recess taken away. I let go of the bitterness and reminded myself to be grateful that with Anne's guidance, I'd talked my way out of PE/study hall and into the TA position. Anne really knew how to work the system.

Her argument, which I copied and pasted from her e-mail into one addressed to my guidance counselor and memorized to get my parents' approval, argued that I'd had more art classes under my belt than any other student and "teacher's assistant" would look good on my otherwise skimpy college applications. My first-choice school was still the Art Institute of Chicago, so the powers that be, both at school and at home, relented and allowed me to take on the position.

This was cool for many reasons. The biggest being that one of the students taking the class was none other than self-professed Art King, David Jenkins. I got a smug little thrill each day when he took his spot at one of the studio tables like a commoner, while I took mine on the wobbly stool in the front.

David and I had been competing in every art competition and event since freshman year. He edged me out for last year's annual citywide show. Each school could place only one artist in the show, so I was out of luck. The $250 prize was cool, but the real thrill was the exposure. Foster Neuwirth came in from New York City every year to act as the judge. She was a Very Big Deal in the art world and came here only because it was her hometown. A nod from Foster Neuwirth could do wonders for your ego . . . and your acceptance into an elite art school, as she sat on the board of the Art Institute.

Even worse than losing our school's only spot last year to David Jenkins was the fact that he won. He won the whole citywide art show, and he was only a junior! Sure, it might have been *my* secret plot. But when he pulled it off, it just seemed tacky. This is when he assumed the crown—and that he was a better artist than me. But as Anne and I liked to say, if you assume, you make an Art King out of you and me.

The pizza in my journal had gone from smiling to smirking and now wore a crown. I slid down in my seat and worked on stoking up some pencil-lead flames in a giant doodled pizza oven.

"Ouch. Who are we setting on fire today?" Anne flopped into the seat next to me and dropped a Ziploc bag of baby carrots on the table next to a tub of hummus. "BP, baby." She sighed in frustration at my blank look. "BP? Betterment Plan?"

"Oh, right, sure. Me, too." I pointed down at my plate of broccoli.

"I'm sorry, but having the lunch lady smother your vegetables with a ladle of congealed nacho-cheeselike substance pretty much wipes out any BP aspect of your meal."

I pushed the plate away. Her observation, though gross, rang true.

She leaned over and nodded in recognition at my doodle. "Ah, *David*. You are so talented. You really captured him. Maybe you should do a study of portraits in pepperoni for your admission portfolio. Mom clipped some of the Helga/Elvis shots from the paper that you could stick in there. Isn't that what those artsy types like? You could make out like it's some weird modern art political statement."

"That's not really my style," I said.

That was the problem. I didn't really have a style yet. I couldn't even decide what kind of art I wanted to concentrate on. Anne had it easy. She was focused, if not driven. The current object of her focus was a guy named Erik sitting at the drama table across the aisle.

"Erik? A theater guy?" I raised my eyebrows. "This is new."

"He goes by 'T-Shirt' now."

I muffled my snort in deference to her obvious deep feelings for the guy.

"He's usually the stage manager. It's not like he's up there doing the acting or anything. And lugging around all those sets sure does a body good," she said.

Anne suggestively swigged her bottle of flavored protein water and zoned in on him. He looked up midsentence from talking with some blonde like he'd lost his train of thought. The girl with MARIA, the name of the female lead, printed across her back, turned and shot Anne a nasty look. Having disrupted the world enough for the moment, Anne cracked up and went back to her carrots.

"But isn't he directing the show or something? Sounds pretty theater-ish to me. I thought you had a strict no-drama, no-wrestlers, no-debate-team rule," I said.

"Sure. I mean, while there are obvious benefits to the athleticism of the sport of wrestling, who can get past those weird outfits they wear? Ick. I'm sorry, but no one wants to see that. And a debate team guy would be such a drag. I like winning my arguments without having to put out a whole lot of effort. The 'no drama' rule, however, has a little wiggle room." Anne pointed to the departing T-Shirt. "Besides, he only went for the assistant director job so he could wear the T-shirt around school. You have to respect a guy who can think ahead."

I watched T-Shirt dump his tray. A bright white stenciled, ASS. DIRECTOR stood out across the broad back of his *The Sound of Music* T-shirt.

"Maria" scurried after him, dumping her own barely touched tray and shooting Anne a smug smile over one shoulder as she slid her hand into the back pocket of his Levi's. Erik looked down in surprise and then shrugged and returned the gesture.

"Classy." I rolled my eyes.

Anne hummed a few perfectly pitched bars of the song "How Do You Solve a Problem Like Maria" and batted her eyelashes with exaggerated innocence. "Gosh, I bet T-Shirt, being a theater buff, would enjoy our gig this weekend. Perhaps I should invite him. I'm sure he has a friend he can bring."

I groaned at the reminder. "Explain to me again how we ended up filling in for someone at a professional dinner theater? And why I'm the one doing the acting when you are clearly the true genius in that category?" Anne might never have deigned to step foot on stage, but the girl didn't make it through a solid two hours of her life without acting her way into, or out of, trouble.

"I told you, you don't have to act, you have to *react*. It's really more of a set job than anything. Besides, it was my connection that landed the job, and I'm doing my part by getting us the boys. It won't look believable unless we bring dates. It's one little momentary bit of time in the spotlight, and you're done. Free dinner, fifty bucks each, and we're that much closer to our dream dresses. It'll be fun. And showing that little upstart who she's messing with ain't a bad bonus."

"Erik, now, is it?"

"T-Shirt."

"Whatever. It's still not like you to go for someone remotely close to our age. Whatever happened to that guy Chad?"

Anne waved a carrot stick in dismissal. "You had a point. If I'm serious about earning this money, I simply don't have the free time to be running around with random guys all of the time. And it's far too soon to even guess who I might want to go to prom with, so the whole exercise would be fun, but pointless. Until prom, chasing boys will be strictly limited to school hours."

"You are so disciplined," I said.

"It's impressive, isn't it?"

"Except, we don't have after-school jobs anymore," I reminded her.

"That's where you're wrong. I heard about a job for female models and signed us up. You don't even have to have experience! Amateurs are welcome—"

"OMG, are you insane? That's it. We are going straight home from school today. With your seven hundred channels, there's bound to be at least three or four 'after-school specials' on."

"Excuse me? Remember who got the thirty-four on the ACT. And still you think that I'm stupid?" Anne said.

"Well, 'amateur female models wanted' is code for 'come and let me talk you out of your clothes and plaster the photos across the Internet—oh, and transportation included . . . in the trunk of my car.' I hope you didn't actually give them our real names."

"Real names, phone numbers, and measurements, actually. I had to guess at yours—"

"Anne!"

"Calm down, Quigley. It's not what you think. Really, you need to cut back on the caffeine or something. Mumsy

Dear is volunteering at the Rhode Island School of Design's Fashion Institute one night a week. Some of her students need warm bodies to try their projects on as they design. They use those adjustable mannequin things for the early stages, but she wants them to see their creations in motion."

"Oh. Well, that sounds pretty cool."

"Told you I'd hook us up. It's every Wednesday night from six to nine, and you can ride in with the queen of sateen herself. Ten bucks an hour to sit around waiting for some fashion geek to plaster us with chiffon. You can even bring your homework, since you seem so fond of doing the stuff."

"I'm just fond of graduating and getting out of this town. Not all of us can memorize the entire textbook an hour before the exam and ace it."

"Oops! That reminds me."

I went back to my notebook as Anne checked her watch and pulled out her chem textbook. The Art King pizza got a last-minute reprieve as I used my pencil of fiery death to multiply the number of Wednesdays left before prom instead. If Ms. Parisi needed us for the whole semester, we'd be only seventy dollars short of our goal. The whole pizza fiasco had set us back. Not only did we lose our jobs, but the guy had charged us for all the returned pizzas. Six afternoons of heinous hairnets and instead of a paycheck, we were down thirty-eight bucks apiece.

"Done!" Anne slammed the cover of her textbook shut.

"What? That was only like ten minutes, tops."

"Oops, better hurry then. My brain only keeps the info for about three times as long as I spent memorizing it. Is that a number-two pencil?"

Anne plucked the pencil out of my hand and ran toward the cafeteria exit to download everything from her megabrain onto some unsuspecting exam sheet. The bell rang, signaling the whopping four minutes they gave us to get from one end of school to the other. I sighed and dragged myself up to head for the art building. At least I had my wobbly stool to look forward to.

• • • • • • • • • • • •

"Where are they?" I asked Anne for the eighth time since we walked into the dinner theater. "This place is packed and the show should start any minute. I haven't even been told what I'm supposed to do."

"Relax. If T-Shirt says they'll be here, they'll be here. His friend Brian got busted in his dad's car for not speeding through a yellow quick enough—"

"You mean, running a red?" Anne's grasp of the rules of the road was frightening at best.

"Details. Anyway, T had to scrounge up someone else to bring last minute."

"Great. Nothing like feeling even more pathetic."

"It's not really a date—this is just work. I'm going to run out and see if they're in the parking lot."

Anne slid easily between the round tables dotting the floor and scooted for the exit. Our table sat up front and center since I'd be helping with some as-yet-unnamed element of the action. A woman dressed all in black with a tiny headset motioned to me from behind the stage curtain to meet her by the side door. I looked around and hustled over, trying to be discreet.

"I'm sorry, was I supposed to wear all black?" I asked.

"What? No, you're fine. Walk with me so we don't attract much attention. We have the Poe Society here tonight, full house. Very demanding connoisseurs of this type of show, their approval will do great things for our company."

We wandered out through a side door into a secret hallway from the kitchen to the theater. Waiters bustled back and forth with ominously smoking trays filled with ruby-red cocktails.

"Dry ice," the woman explained. "Just a few drops of

water on a little piece in the middle of the tray—it gets the audience in the mood."

"Ah. I just thought in all black I'd blend in while I'm moving whatever you need me to. Or is it just a matter of placing a dagger or bottle of poison somewhere strategic without people noticing? Anne said I didn't have to actually act. I'm not an actor."

"Oh, I think you can handle this," the woman chuckled. "So Victoria's daughter didn't tell you what you'd be doing? Classic."

Her peal of laughter set off a fluttering in my stomach. "Wait. What exactly am I doing?"

"Simple. Our dead body called in sick."

I tried to concentrate on her instructions. They'd be setting down rolls and butter as the show started. Then the salad course. Mine would arrive sans dressing and then a shot would ring out. A spotlight would land on me right as I faceplanted into my romaine. I tried to memorize her advice to chow down on the rolls so my stomach wouldn't growl from the tempting smells as everyone else ate, and to make sure I adjusted the lettuce to leave a decent-sized breathing space so I didn't get claustrophobic. To dodge the single cherry tomato added for effect as I landed. It was just all so hard to remember when my brain was fully engaged in hating Anne. I tuned back in as the woman finished explaining the story line of the murder mystery.

"So that's it. At the end, the main characters will come retrieve you from your seat and do a *Weekend at Bernie's* routine—you know, the dancing corpse number. Don't worry, they're fantastic. Just keep your eyes closed and let them flop your body around. Then, lights will come down and you come back to life to do a proper curtain call as one of our performers!"

Music swelled from inside the theater as the waiters reemerged with empty trays.

"Oops, better get in there! Follow this hall to the end and take a left. You can enter the theater from the back."

I numbly headed down the hall.

"Oh, Quigley?"

I turned, hoping she'd laugh and reveal it was all some elaborate prank.

"Break a leg!"

I turned back toward the theater, thinking of the patterned tights I'd admired on my best friend during the drive over. "Yeah. I think I just might know whose."

I crouched down and headed toward our table in the

darkened theater as the actors performed an opening number. The silhouettes of three people sat at the table, so at least our dates had arrived.

I slid into my seat and leaned into Anne, who cut me off. "I'm so sorry. I had no idea, Quigley. I swear. I promise I'll make this up to you."

"You *totally* knew, the set lady told me. Now switch places with me and you do this or there's going to be more than one dead body at this table."

"I can't," she hissed back. "We're already in our places and they said the dead body had to sit in that particular chair. If we move now, everyone will notice and it will wreck the whole show. We need this cash and you know how I feel about acting. Where's your sense of humor? I thought you'd think this was hilarious."

"Oh, really? So why were you apologizing then?"

I grabbed the last of the rolls from the departing waiter's tray and took an angry bite.

"That's not what I was apologizing for," she said with a look of genuine remorse. "That is."

I followed her gaze across the table to the smirking grin of none other than David Jenkins, the Art King himself. He waggled his fingers at me.

I was still choking on the bite of roll and trying to breathe as the waiter delivered our salads. Being unable to speak might have been a blessing since my brain in its fury wasn't forming too many coherent words. T-Shirt, wearing his nicest YOU SAY TOMATO, I SAY TOMATO—IT DOESN'T REALLY MAKE MUCH SENSE WHEN YOU READ IT shirt under a sports coat, offered me his water, while David just laughed himself stupid.

"Ewww, what is this?" Anne asked, poking at the thick pool of blue cheese dressing smothering her greens. "This is so not BP."

She reached across and swapped our plates with a conciliatory smile. "This is way more your style—go for it. You deserve it tonight."

The shot echoed through the theater and a hot blast of spotlight landed square on my face. I looked down, horrified, and gave a very convincing performance of someone about to meet her death as I flopped into my plate of creamy dressing, forgetting, until the moment it met my forehead with a sickening squish, to dodge the cherry tomato.

Chapter Three

· ·

I could hear the clink of my parents' silverware in the dining room as I stood at the door watching for Anne's mom. The urge to kill my good friend for the dinner theater fiasco died when she borrowed the Art King's cell at lunch, pretending to want to show off his *Quigley's Body* film of me being tossed around stage with lettuce and croutons glued to my cheeks and, instead, deleted it forever. It also helped that the rash from the acid of the cherry tomato had finally faded from my forehead.

My family was probably the last one left in America who actually sat down to dinner together every night. Anne thought it was cool, but I'd have traded for her brie-with-crackers or Thai-takeout-in-front-of-the-TV life, any day.

I pulled at the shoulder strap of the bikini Anne had lent me. She claimed that it was "one size fits all" since the straps just tied at whatever length you needed. I probably could have fit one cheek into the narrow cloth at the back meant for both of Anne's. But Anne didn't believe in one-piece suits, and we needed to wear something so we could get fitted without flashing half of her mom's design class. I'd have to find a time when Mom was out of the house to go digging through the summer storage up in the attic.

I decided not to go into a lot of detail about the job over dinner. My parents were already a little edgy over my hanging out with Ms. Parisi. Her frequent jaunts to Milan and Madrid when Anne was little were not my folks' idea of proper motherhood. Even the fact that she'd scaled back once her career took off and had done a complete one-eighty, discipline-wise, after Anne's first brush with trouble at school didn't help her reputation with them.

Fortunately, I'd convinced my parents that Anne had taken the fall for the real troublemakers—that there was no way a lowly freshman could pull off rewriting an entire student newspaper not only to feature several teachers in compromising stories but also to announce a water main break–induced day off from school that the student population was all too eager to honor. I'd kept a straight face while proclaiming my friend's innocence, despite the coincidence that each of the teachers Photoshopped into the home-ec sweatshop-ring article had recently reprimanded her timeliness-challenged ways.

I thought, mom-wise, Ms. Parisi did pretty good, considering her history. It can't be easy having to see the face of your kid's secret biological father plastered across the cover of the "sexiest man alive" issue of every other publication on the news rack. I was one of the few people in the whole world Anne had let in on her parentage and was under threat of death if I ever let it slip. Her parents had a onetime fling at a runway show when her dad was just an unknown model straight from the cornfields of Iowa. She liked to say she got her good looks from her dad and her taste in guys from her mom.

I thought she got a lot of other good things from her mom, like her independence and her crazy impressive smarts. Not that I would say that to her right now. Anne hadn't dealt with the crackdown of supervision with a whole lot of grace. She was currently using the majority of her brilliance to find the most cutting things possible to say to Ms. Parisi. This was in revenge for the injustice of having a curfew—a phenomenon that had neatly escaped Anne so far in life.

The headlights of Ms. Parisi's convertible lit up the hall.

"They're here! I'll be back by ten," I called over my shoulder.

Anne was sitting in the backseat, flipping through a magazine in the dark. Ms. Parisi smiled and patted the front seat.

"Hey, Anne. Hi, Ms. Parisi," I said.

"Victoria, dear. I tell you every time I see you, just call me Victoria. Ms. Parisi is so formal," she said. She clicked a button on the dash and pulled back into my cul-de-sac.

"It's not her fault her parents did a good job raising her. She's respectful to her *elders*," Anne said.

I hid my smile at Anne's unconscious slam to her own manners. Ms. Parisi ignored her, smiling and patting my knee. I wiggled a little as the heated seat kicked in. Sitting in Ms. Parisi's car always made me feel like I'd peed myself. Ms. Parisi turned up the perfect digital speakers to cover the lack of conversation as we headed down the highway into the city.

. . . .

The studio was filled with twelve tall tables. Each held one student, a pile of fabric swatches, and half-formed dress pieces. All twenty-four eyes were glued on Ms. Parisi as she strolled into the room and dropped her bag lightly on the table in front. Hero worship hung thick in the air. True fashion lovers appreciated her historical body of work, but her stint as judge on a popular design-based reality show had thrown her into a whole new category of celebrity.

I had invited Anne over to watch the show with my parents, who tolerated it so as not to be rude to my friend. I hoped their seeing Ms. Parisi's evenhanded and thoughtful way of critiquing even the most bizarre designs, not to mention designers, would impress them and let them see her in a new light. Unfortunately, Anne's ridiculing and snarky jokes throughout her mom's appearances pretty much made it a wash.

"Good evening, designers." Ms. Parisi smiled graciously.

The faces of the students lit up at the title. They leaned toward her like she was some sort of magnet. I expected applause to spontaneously erupt at any minute. I couldn't imagine what it must be like inspiring that kind of reaction from a group of strangers. Anne rolled her eyes and flopped into a chair along the wall. I sat beside her and tried to guess which one of the guys Anne would go for first.

"As I mentioned last week, I brought in some live models for you to get a better feel for the movement in your designs. They will be joining us for the class throughout the semester and will be at your disposal for fittings and draping exercises. I'd like to introduce Anne and Quigley."

Ms. Parisi motioned us up to the front. I gave a shy little half wave. Anne stepped forward and struck a dramatic pose.

"Hello, everyone. I'm sure you will all enjoy Mother's class," Anne said.

Ms. Parisi's perfectly made-up mouth tightened the tiniest bit at Anne's exaggerated *Mother*. Anne beamed at the audible gasps. She looked a lot less pleased with the flood of "you look way too young to have a daughter that age" compliments that followed. Ms. Parisi bowed a little thank-you and quickly moved on.

"As you can see, these lovely young ladies have very different body types. This should enable you to find a good match for whatever you are working on this semester. I'll be handing out a lesson plan with your objectives for this week, as well as the girls' measurements. But first, I'd like to test your eye for figure. This will be important when you are in a position to pick and choose your models. You'll need to guesstimate who would work well for what is in your mind's eye. I'd like you all to take out paper and pencil and write your estimates of bust, waist, hips, inseam, and shoulder to waist for each of the girls as they appear in their street clothes."

My face flamed as twelve sets of eyes shot to my body. They looked from head to toe with concentration, sizing me up. I wished I'd refused my mother's signature pork chops and just had the green-bean-and-mushroom-soup casserole at dinner. Or that I had at least worn my jeans without the frayed waistband. That frayed denim must add at least a half inch. Maybe more.

Anne seemed to have no such concerns and stood with one hip thrust forward, allowing her already low-slung jeans to slide an inch lower. Her gaze had landed on a guy with black spiky hair. He had what looked like a dog collar around his neck. A strategic rip in his shirt revealed a tribal armband tattoo. Anne's interest had not escaped the notice of Ms. Parisi, whose perfectly shaped brows were wrinkled in the tiniest frown of dismay.

The students looked up, one by one, as they completed the task. Ms. Parisi circled the room, nodding and pointing down at their sheets.

"Very good. Here are the girls' actual measurements—take a look and see where you might have erred a bit," she said.

I blushed again as the class looked from the paper to my

body and made notes and adjustments. I was beginning to wonder whether I had let go of the pizza-making dream a little too soon.

"Now go ahead and pull out your designs from last week to see which of the girls will better work to model your dress. May I have a show of hands as to who will be using Anne this week?"

I cringed as all twelve hands shot up. This was like gym class. A guy with wavy, light brown hair looked around and yanked his hand back down.

"Okay, then. Alexander, will you be needing Quigley for your fitting?"

"Yes. Sorry, I just got their names mixed up."

I breathed a sigh of relief. At least it wasn't total and complete rejection. Just an eleven out of twelve rejection. Anne squeezed my hand.

"It's only because they were doing sheath dresses last week—you know, boobs need not apply," she whispered.

I tried to give her a genuine smile back. I really didn't have any major problems with my body, but getting scrutinized standing next to Anne could give anybody a complex. Anne made a beeline for The Spikester, and I wandered over to Alexander's table.

"Hi. I'm Quigley."

"Cool name. You can just call me Zander. Do you want to see what I'm working on?"

I pulled up a stool and sat down. Normally, a guy as good looking as he was would have me stammering and tripping over my feet. But he had such a laid-back manner, it was like I was hanging out with family.

"See this? The fabric hangs over here and then gets bunched into a shirred bustline," he said.

I nodded politely. But in reality, the whole drawing had a sort of bunched look to it. I wasn't sure what he was going for, but if I had to choose one word for his design, it would have to be *stumpy*. I was starting to feel less than complimented that he chose me for a model. He suddenly threw down his pencil and hung his head in his hands.

"I know. It's terrible," he moaned.

"Um, nooo. No, it's just—"

"Terrible. Terrible! It's all a bunch of crap."

"No, I wouldn't say *crap* exactly."

I tried to tear my eyes away from the overly bright red and fuchsia blob on his sketch pad. The arms and legs he had added for reference had a definite Picasso-esque quality about them. He took a deep breath and let it out slowly through pursed lips. He met my concerned gaze and shrugged with a chuckle.

"Such a drama queen, aren't I?" He dropped the offending sketch pad into my hands. "Here, let me show you the actual dress."

Anne was across the aisle, leaning not so subtly into The Spikester as he laid a swatch of black lace across her shoulder. Ms. Parisi was doing a fair job of pretending she wasn't hovering over the edgy designer's shoulder. When I turned back to Zander, I almost dropped his sketch pad. What he held up was a fluid dream in crimson with such a subtle touch of purple that is seemed to glow.

"Wow."

Zander's eyebrows shot up in relief. "Really?"

"Oh my God, yes! Oh, I want that."

Zander laughed, but I was dead serious. I set his sketchbook down to pull the skirt out for a better look. Zander sighed as he caught sight of the awful blob on his sketchbook. I sighed as I saw that the dress was going to be a good six inches too small for me. I'd have said I would be six inches too big, but I preferred to think of the dress as being to blame. It was my own version of the glass half-full/half-empty distinction.

Zander stared down at the sketch. "Hopeless."

"Hopeless." I agreed and let the shimmery silk slide out of my fingers.

We sat there for a minute lost in mutual misery until the clicking of Ms. Parisi's approaching heels snapped us out of it. She always wore shoes with super-long, skinny toes that reminded me of the legs under the fallen Oz house. They cost a fortune and were in all the fashion mags, so I guess "witchy" was in, and I just had no taste in footwear.

"How are we doing here?"

"Oh, good. Fine. Just need to make a few adjustments," Zander stammered, and leaned over to hide his sketchbook.

Ms. Parisi stroked the dress. "Beautiful choice of fabrics, Alexander. You have a good eye for movement." She cocked her head and slid her hand inside the dress and nodded. "Smart to leave a decent seam allowance. It's delicate material; be sure not to damage it when making your alterations. This color will look lovely on Quigley."

"I agree," said Zander.

Ms. Parisi's radar went off at Anne's giggle. Across the room, The Spikester was taking Anne's waist measurement as she pretended to be ticklish. Ms. Parisi's witchy shoes clicked off to intervene before he moved on up to the bust.

"So can you really fix *that* dress to fit *this* body?" I asked.

"Of course." Zander was already turning the garment inside out to inspect the seams.

"I'm sorry you have to do all that. I know I'm not exactly a model figure."

"Are you kidding? You have a great figure—perfect proportions. Today's model figures are pretty warped, if you ask me. Look at how tiny your waist is—to tell the truth, hourglass is a great look for this style of dress. You're actually helping me out—helping me envision how much better it can be."

My cheeks probably matched the dress. "It's still a lot of work."

"Sure, but *this*"—he flipped the skirt with grin—"I'm good at." He glanced at the sketchbook in disgust. "That, on the other hand . . ."

"Well, the final product is what matters. Right?"

"I wish that was all that mattered. I just can't seem to translate what I see in my head to what my hands draw on paper."

I sat back down on the stool and flipped through the rest of his sketchbook. I searched for something to compliment. When he was engrossed with his little thread picker, I turned several of the pages to the side, and even upside down, trying to figure out what garment the sketch was supposed to be. He was right—hopeless.

"You, umm, choose really beautiful colors?"

He looked up and laughed. It was so genuine I couldn't help but laugh with him.

"That's like saying my dresses have really great personalities," he gasped.

This set me off on another round of giggles. The class had turned to see what was so funny. We tried to compose ourselves. Zander was still chuckling as he went back to his seam snipping.

I turned to a fresh sheet in his sketchbook and picked up a red pencil. The lines of his gown flared out, and I added a swoop of purple here and there where the material would catch the light. I exaggerated the length of the limbs and neck of the figure with a thick black line. Satisfied, I picked up the red pencil again and started coloring.

This was turning out to be the best job ever.

. . . .

Chapter Four

Mrs. Albertt's voice droned on and on about processing times and F-stops. The tangy smell of developing chemicals wafted from the darkroom. I jerked out of my near doze and wondered if they were related to chloroform. I heard you had to contact the government for proper disposal of toxic substances, which did not make the thought of hours spent elbow deep in the stuff very enticing.

I shifted in my seat trying to keep myself awake with the little clicks that sounded each time the stool leg hit the ugly green linoleum. David's voice snapped me out of my daze.

"This is fascinating, Mrs. Albertt. So we can purposefully overexpose our pieces for effect?" he asked.

"Suck up," I said under my breath.

Everyone knew this particular class was a complete waste. Only at an arts-dedicated charter school would a course devoted to only film and prints even exist. The future of photography was digital. Nobody did print work anymore. But Mrs. Albertt was a technophobe purist when it came to photography. David would surely find some way to wow her. It was all politics.

"Exactly, David!" Mrs. Albertt beamed. "The citywide show our very own David won last year will feature a new category—art photography. Maybe as the semester progresses, some of you might try your hand at the type of effect David was just asking about."

The bell interrupted Mrs. Albertt's David-adoration. I hopped off my stool and headed for the theater to track down Anne. She'd become a regular drama convert in the past few weeks since T-Shirt had caught her eye. I'd have worried she was actually getting serious about one guy, if not for the weekly reassurance to the contrary, courtesy of The Spikester.

As the other designers continued to choose Anne's waif-like look over my, ahem, sturdier build, Zander stuck by me. And, occasionally, into me. But the prick of fitting pins was part of life as a model. We had settled into a comfortable Wednesday night friendship. He'd play with fabric and the physical lines of his garment; I'd redraw the blobs in his sketchbook to resemble whatever he was actually working on. During the week he'd use my sketches to practice his own drawing skills. So it wasn't *really* like cheating or anything.

I almost felt bad taking the thirty bucks a night for having such a good time, but Ms. Parisi didn't seem to mind. Though she might have been preoccupied trying to keep a handle on the abundance of fittings The Spikester seemed to require of his all-too-willing model.

She handled it quite well when Anne, while being pinned by The Spikester, nearly experienced a wardrobe malfunction with the neck string on her bikini. Ms. Parisi had pounced before anything was revealed and pulled the strings back into a double knot as tight as her smile. The poor woman had nerves of steel.

"What's so funny?"

I jumped as David's arrogant drawl cut through my thoughts.

"Why are you following me?" I snapped at him, embarrassed.

"I didn't realize I was. You own the halls now?"

I sped up and turned down the empty hall to the auditorium. I'd blown my physics test that morning and had a meeting with my guidance counselor after school. My day needed no further challenges, particularly in the form of dealing with David. I heard the echo of his feet still following me. The only thing down this hall was the theater.

I spun around to face him. "*What* do you want?"

"What do I want?" David took a step closer and lowered his voice. "I want you, Quigley. You're a pretty girl. You'd make a nice Art *Queen*. What do you say?"

My heart pounded as a mini-gasp slipped out. Maybe the residue of developer fumes on his way-too-close body had clouded my brain. I struggled in vain for a response for several eternally long seconds.

He pulled back and laughed at me as I stammered in shock. "Or maybe, just maybe, I want to get back to the sets I'm painting for the play." He sauntered past me chuckling. "It's not always about you, Quigley. You should work on that whole self-involvement thing you've got going on."

I stood frozen in a mix of rage and humiliation, wishing I had studied enough physics to know if it was possible for a human being to melt into linoleum. And if so, how I might achieve that. I heard welcoming yells of "Hey, Art King!" and "Art King's here!" echoing from the theater doors.

I turned and headed back down the hall to the cafeteria

instead. *Sorry, Anne. This is so not worth it.* With every class-room I passed, I thought of another good comeback.

That always happened to me. A whole pile of stunners materialized, too late to use them. Self-involved. David thinks I'm self-involved? Unreal. It was during times like these that I felt like counting the days left of high school. That thought just reminded me of my meeting with my guidance counselor.

According to the note, we were supposed to work on a Plan B college entrance strategy. Which sounded suspiciously like teacher code for crappy-student-who-needs-help-to-get-pawned-off-on-some-school-any-school-so-she-doesn't-screw-up-our-placement-ratio. Anne had received telltale fat manila envelopes from three different Ivy League schools. My letters from universities came back in your standard business envelope. It didn't take much room when the letters started, "Thank you for your interest. Unfortunately . . ."

Anne tried to pump me up about the one that included a "waiting list concession" at the very bottom. It was like they didn't even mean it, like an afterthought. Really, it was just that—an afterthought. *After* all the good students *thought* about where they'd attend, they would let me know if they needed a warm body to fill a dorm bed.

It was enough to make a girl want to hit the nacho-cheese broccoli.

I stood in line to pay for my BP-approved lunch instead. I snapped a baby carrot in two, wishing it was one of David's stupid, artistic fingers, and poked the pieces into the blob of hummus on my plate. I smiled at the resemblance to The Spikester's hair.

I selected a few more of the skinnier veggies and soon had a freeform sculpture in progress. I nibbled a piece of carrot into a little orange scowl and nudged it into place. Not bad. Maybe Anne was on to something with that pepperoni idea. I could do a whole series of food portraits. It would be better if the medium fit the personality better, though. The Spikester was so not a carrot-sticks-and-hummus kind of guy.

"I was waiting for ten minutes. What happened to you?" Anne asked.

I pulled my backpack off the saved chair next to me. "Why didn't you tell me that David was working on the play?"

"Well, hello to you, too. Quigley, it's not like you exactly welcome mention of his name. He's a friend of T-Shirt's, remember? When the original set designer bailed, he asked David to fill in. I thought I'd do you a favor and keep that info to myself."

"Well, thanks a lot. I made a total jerk of myself in the hall."

Anne's normal smile turned into the grin that usually landed her in detention. "Not according to David," she sing-songed. "He came in and asked T-Shirt if you were seeing anybody."

I sucked my breath in so quickly that tiny pieces of baby carrot flew the wrong way down my throat.

Anne banged on my hacking, gasping back and giggled. "*Really*, Quigley. You're making a scene now. Unless you're trying to catch David's attention—bet he does a mean Heimlich."

I barked like an unattractive seal with laryngitis and wiped at my watering eyes. "Not funny." I gasped for breath.

Anne ignored my near-death experience and pulled my plate closer. She turned it around and lovingly stroked an orange spike. "I can't wait for Wednesday."

"What is up with you and that guy, anyway?" I asked.

"Which guy?"

With Anne, that was a fair question. "The designer guy. The Spikester. How old is he, anyway?"

"Who knows? Age is in the eye of the beholder—"

"I think that's 'beauty,'" I said.

"Well, he's beautiful, too. He's got the most piercing blue eyes."

"Yeah, he's big into 'piercing.' Besides, it's only the eyeliner that makes his eyes so intense."

"Well, say what you like—it's called style. And even you have to admit his eyebrow ring is way hot. So, I guess he's twenty-two or something. He said he was seventeen when his son was born and he's going into kindergarten soon—"

"Oh my God! He's got a kid? A kid who's *five?*"

"Almost five. Dude, why are you freaking out? A lot of people have kids who are five."

"Not a lot of people who you're crazy in love with." Anne's was the snort heard around the world, or at least around the cafeteria. "Well, you know what I mean. You are totally into the guy."

"Sure, he's cool. And probably going to be the next Marc Ecko, or something. But for now, we're keeping it cas'."

"Ah, so your mom caught on?"

Anne pouted and scraped the last bit from her yogurt cup. "Totally. I'm guessing she made it clear that if he wanted to pass the class, he'd better *not* make a pass at me. What a killjoy. You're so lucky your mom's not around to see you and Alexander."

"Me and Zander? We're not together."

"Yeah, right. You guys spend three hours together every week in your own little world, laughing your rapidly dwindling gluteus maximus off. For the past six weeks he's never once picked me to model his stuff."

I smiled at her compliment and made a mental note to check out the full-length mirror later. I'd been so wrapped up in tight-roping that thin line between Cs and Ds in my classes, I'd completely spaced that there was some practical reason for Anne's Betterment Plan.

"From *that* you get that we're together-together? In case you don't remember, spending three hours together every week is my job. It's not my fault no one else ever wants me to wear their clothes."

"Well, you sure seem to be enjoying your job. It's like your own private comedy club back there. And he makes you the most gorgeous dresses. Don't get me wrong—The Spikester's look is hot. That bodice made entirely of metal zippers might have looked cool, but his fashion can be a little painful."

I accepted half of Anne's offered banana. The carrots and hummus had lost their appeal after being transformed into the face of The Spikester. "Well, you must suffer for your beauty, after all. Zander's great—really funny and so sweet.

But it's not like that with us—we're friends. I do love his work. But it's not like he's designing the gowns for *me* or anything."

"Are you sure about that? Every one is your style, only more fab. Colors that rock with your exact skin tone. He spends half the class drooling over your drawings like they're Rembrandts or something."

"He's trying to learn from them."

"Imitation is the highest form of flattery, Quigley. Not that I disapprove. Zander's definitely worthy. And you need someone to keep David on his toes, anyway."

"What!"

"Well, you can't give too much power to a guy—keep a few on the line and they all appreciate you a lot more. It's really the only way to run a successful relationship."

I leaned back and tried to remember if any of Anne's successful relationships had made it past the one-month mark.

"So, really, this is perfect," Anne went on. "You just need to decide between your guys before prom. I wouldn't even bother to think too hard about it until a few weeks before the dance."

"Between my guys?"

"Sure. David and Zander. You can't be greedy, Quigley. Come prom time you'll have to decide which one to keep and which to let go. Nobody's that much of a jerk—you know David's only being mean because he's into you. Boys are dumb like that."

I stared at her pupils to see if she'd stood too close to a Bunsen burner in chem. "Anne. I don't have to decide which guy to keep. I don't even have *one* guy, much less two."

"Well, prom's less than six weeks away. Who are you going to go with then, Quigley?"

I felt a hollow burning in my stomach that I couldn't blame on the hummus. It was a good question. The money saving was right on track. The guy situation—not so much. "Look, Zander is just a friend, and he's totally not interested in me like that."

"Well, maybe the David thing will work out. I know you have a weird history, but I was serious about him asking T-Shirt if you were with anyone."

I tried a light laugh, but it came out a little too harsh. "Come on. David? No. Never. I can't stand him. He's a pompous jerk, besides being a no-talent art hack. Real attractive qualities, Anne."

Anne's mouth dropped, and I instantly knew what I would see if I followed her eyes behind me. I steeled myself before turning to the Art King himself. Except he didn't look much like the Art King.

David's usual cocky smile was a little crooked. "Wow. I guess that probably means you don't want to catch the new exhibit Saturday." He laid the brochure from the Contemporary Art Museum down next to The Spikester sculpture. "At least not with me. But, umm, you should check it out. It's a new collection of digital photography. I just, you know, thought you'd like it or something." He shrugged and tried another smile that didn't make it to his eyes before walking quickly away.

The prickle of oncoming tears hit my eyes as my cheeks burned.

"Whoa. Brutal," Anne said.

I grabbed my plate and stalked to the trash can. I shook it three times, but the stupid hummus was like glue. "I didn't mean—I mean, if I'd known he was there I would have never—"

"I know," Anne said quietly. "I never would have pegged him as the sensitive type. But wowza—he really looked hurt, didn't he?"

"Yes, Anne. I caught that." I finally just threw the whole stupid plate in the trash. I returned to the table and slammed my chair back in, then grabbed my bag. "I gotta go."

Chapter Five

· · · · · · · · · · · · · · · · · · · ·

I looked up after hearing Zander's sigh. He patiently
replaced the sash I had let slip for the second time within two
minutes. He took a step back and gave a little nod. He pulled
one of the pins held between his pursed lips and fastened the
sash an inch higher. "Mwaming mwong?"

"Huh?"

He pulled the last two pins from his mouth. "Something
wrong?"

"Ha. Something? Everything. Everything wrong."

"Bad day?"

"Try bad week. Bad month. Bad year."

"Hmm. Drama queen is usually more *my* style," he said.

I smiled. "Stop. I don't want cheering up. I'm enjoying my
misery."

"Okay, then. As you were."

I flounced onto his stool, forgetting I was wearing his

project for the week. I jumped back up at his moan and tried to recrimp the poof of petticoats under the back half of the short skirt.

"Are you sure a bustle is the right look for my body type? I mean, I have a pretty good bustle going on, *au naturel*."

"I'm going to forgive you for insulting my creation, Quigley, since you are so obviously distraught. But if you will just join me at the mirror, I would at least like to show you how dead wrong you are."

I motioned over to Anne, who was standing dead still as The Spikester knelt at her feet and inched a scissors upward for a dramatic jagged slit in the otherwise pristinely sleek white gown. "Now Anne, on the other hand, she could maybe do with a bustle—"

Ms. Parisi hovered near the pair, pretending to inspect the bodice of a dress at a neighboring table.

"Anne couldn't pull off this dress." Zander lowered his voice for Ms. Parisi's benefit. "Not even with The Spikester's help."

My snort of laughter made several other designers look up from their sketch pads.

"Oops, sorry. That probably broke the whole leave-me-to-my-misery mood," he said.

"It's not funny! I did a really jerky thing the other day and I haven't been able to undo it."

Zander grabbed my hips with a little frown and turned me slowly in front of the mirror. "I have a hard time imagining you doing anything 'jerky.' And if you did, whoever it was directed at probably deserved it."

I stared at the unimaginably tiny waist the dress created and resisted the urge to crouch down to see if it was one of those warped funhouse mirrors. Weeks had passed, and I still wasn't used to Zander's magic with a needle and thread.

"So what did this cretin do to inspire your uncharacteristic act of 'jerkiness'?" he asked.

I sighed and headed back to the workstation. "He asked me out."

Zander's eyebrows went up. "Oh?"

We usually sat next to each other happily sketching and stitching in silence for an hour, but something about the sudden quiet between us felt strained. I fidgeted in his creation and felt a weird urge to take back my comment.

He picked at a thread holding on a tiny crystal bead. "So. What did you say?"

"Exactly?"

His forehead wrinkled as he stared at the thread. "Sure." He really seemed preoccupied with that bead.

"I believe I called him a pompous jerk and a no-talent art hack."

Zander's laughter echoed throughout the room.

"It's not funny!"

"It kind of is." Zander wheezed and tried to control himself. "Man, you're brutal. Did he ask you to a hotel or something?" He waved away my glare. "Sorry! Just trying to figure out what sort of invitation gets a guy that type of response."

"Actually, he asked me to the new exhibit of digital photography at the Contemporary Art Museum."

"The nerve!" Zander grinned and lifted my hand to spin me in a twirl. He was suddenly in far too chipper a mood.

"Shut up. It wasn't that. That exhibit is supposed to be really cool. It's just him. I can't stand him—the guy just makes me mental."

"Apparently. So this exhibit . . . is it supposed to be good?"

I went back to check out Zander's sketch of the couture wedding dress. The gorgeous tulip-petal-layered front looked more like two bubbles plopped over a set of legs with all the curviness of a couple of fish sticks. I worried Zander's drawing skills might not come around in time for the final project. That design would have to be created and sketched in the classroom under Ms. Parisi's watchful eye. No help from stray well-meaning models.

"Yeah. That's the stupid thing. I really wanted to go. Not with him or anything. But my parents are tied up with their kids' charity stuff on the weekends, and they're not too big on me wandering around Providence on my own." I pointed at his sketch. "This top half's not bad."

Zander took the gummy gray blob of eraser and started clearing the sketch pad of the bottom scribble. "Soooo—"

"Nope. That's your job," I joked.

He gave me a weak smile before staring at the pad and erasing with incredible concentration. "So, maybe we should go check out this exhibit."

"We? Me and you? Sure, that'd be awesome."

He stopped erasing with a smile. "Wow. That was easy."

"Easy?"

"Well, sure. I was preparing myself for the whole 'no-talent art hack' tirade." He picked up the sketchbook and blew the eraser fragments away. "And in the case of this drawing, it would even be justified."

I laughed. "Don't worry. I try to save that for guys who are asking me out on dates."

"Oh." He stared back at the blank sketchbook. "Right—gotcha."

"Oh no! You erased the whole thing. Now you'll have to start from scratch."

Zander sighed. "Story of my life."

· · · · · · · · · · · ·

I stood outside the auditorium and looked at my watch. It'd been half an hour, but I didn't dare go in to find Anne and risk a run-in with David. My attempts to smooth things over during art class seemed to have gone unnoticed. There was a fine line between taking back my harsh comments without seeming like I was encouraging him, and I'd obviously failed to find it. David's polite smile and lack of eye contact when I approached him in the art room didn't exactly encourage meaningful conversation. So we mostly stuck to chat of the "here's your developing solution" and "I think this is dry now" variety.

I was so embarrassed by my jerkiness, I spent the first two days after the cafeteria scene avoiding him. By the time Anne convinced me just to suck it up and apologize, he was acting like the whole thing had never happened. Maybe I should just let it go, but I almost missed the cocky, obnoxious Art King act. The thought that I'd hurt this new-to-me three-dimensional David was a little much for me to deal with.

I brought it up with my mom just long enough to be reminded why I don't bring up much with my mom. I'm sure her comment that sometimes the toughest people on the out-side were the most sensitive on the inside was well meant, but wasn't exactly comforting. I pushed the niggling ring of truth in the comment away with my trademark fake smile, "Thanks, Mom," and deft change of subject. My parents' world was so solidly black and white, they could never understand that life played across my canvas in a hundred shades of charcoal gray.

I glanced down at my watch again. Enough was enough—I'd have to catch up with Anne later. I was walking down the hall when I heard the door crash open behind me. I stifled a giggle as Anne walked right past me. It was understand-able she might not see me, considering her face was plastered against the assistant director's. Today's little gem—I DON'T THINK MUCH, THEREFORE I MAY NOT BE—stood out on his 100 percent cotton-jersey back as they smooched by.

I cleared my throat. "Um, hello? Best friend here—*patient* best friend?"

Anne pulled herself away, laughing. T-Shirt was still tugging her down the hall as she playfully protested.

"Come on, Anne. Come with us—you haven't been on a single collecting expedition," T-Shirt said. "And this one will be the best yet—full reconnaissance gear, blackened faces— I'll even let you wear my camo pants."

I went to retrieve my friend. "No, thank you. You stay in your pants; she'll stay in hers."

He made a face and pulled Anne back for a last kiss. "Yeah, yeah—*Warden*."

"Oh, you'll be fine without me. Besides, I have to show Quigley my new room décor," Anne said.

T-Shirt grinned. "Oh yeah. Cool. Laters, babe—wish us luck!"

I pulled her down the hall a safe distance from the theater, in case anyone else popped out. "What was that all about?"

"Can't talk here—walls have ears or eyes or whatever. Come on, I'll show you at home. You got your shoes?"

I let my backpack fall to the floor with a groan and sat on the cool linoleum to pull on my track shoes. I hoped the whole Betterment Plan would fall by the wayside as things heated up between Anne and T-Shirt, but since she hadn't decided if he was the one for prom, she was keeping as many options open as possible.

"I heard walking is just about as good for you as jogging," I said after tightening my laces.

"Nice try." Anne was already jogging in place. "Hey—is that David coming?"

I took off in a mini-sprint and let the hall door slam behind me. Anne caught up halfway across the quad.

She grabbed my shoulder and doubled over laughing. "Joking! I was joking. You've really got to do something about that situation. This is a small school and we have the whole rest of the year. That's a long time to be dodging a guy you share half your schedule with."

I kicked a clump of dirt in annoyance and continued on toward Anne's house. "I know. I'll talk to him on Monday."

"Good. I don't think you've blown it entirely."

The jogging made my blood pump loudly in my ears. "I didn't what?"

"Just saying, I think it's salvageable. Guys have big egos, so naturally he had to take a step back. Besides, this might be good. Now he knows you're not going to fall all over him like 'Maria' does."

I shook my head and wondered if an endorphin hit to the brain was the reason none of her words made sense. I slowed as we reached her street. "What are you talking about? And who's Maria?"

"Maria, you know—the blonde. I don't even know her real name—that girl playing the lead in *Sound of Music*. She was all into T-Shirt before I snagged him out from under her. So she moved on to easier prey. No offense."

"David?" I wasn't sure why I suddenly had a knot in my stomach. Must be the run. I'd somehow reached the top of the hill without even noticing.

"Yep. She's been chasing David in the most embarrassing way ever since he signed on to do sets. I mean, holy cow, she's playing Maria! Some nun, huh? Obviously doesn't put much stock into that whole getting-into-character thing." Something in my face put Anne in Mama-tiger mode. "Look, Quigley—you can totally take her. I mean, she's a freshman! The only reason she's even after David, or was after T-Shirt, for that matter, is that she wants to go to prom, and you have to be asked by a senior. Pathetic. Totally pathetic."

"Pathetic," I agreed. I chose not to mention Anne's freshman-year antics when she ended up triple-booked for the dance after spending every afternoon for two months loitering in the senior parking lot. "So David's *with* her?"

"Well, obviously not *too* with her, considering he was asking you out four days ago."

"True." And that was despite little "Maria" making an unholy play for him. Maybe it was the brief glimpse of another side of my longtime foe or my mom's comment, but I caught myself wondering if I had judged him too harshly. He seemed genuine enough when I mangled his attempt to ask me out. . . .

Anne grinned. "Oh my God, you're going to go for him!"

"Am not!" I tried not to smile.

"Are so—you totally are so. I know these things. I'm the expert."

I flopped onto Anne's front steps in defeat. "This is insane. I hate David. I can't stand him. He's a—"

"Pompous jerk and no-talent art hack?" Anne rolled her eyes.

"Shut up."

"So maybe that 'Art King' thing was all an act. Maybe he was jealous of your artistic abilities. Maybe it was all like putting your pigtail into the Indian ink or whatever you art types use."

"India ink. And no. This doesn't add up. He's never paid me any attention, except to make it clear he thinks he's a better artist."

"Well, what would you know? It's not like you've ever had a real boyfriend or anything," Anne said.

She immediately smacked both hands over her mouth. It would have been comical if the comment hadn't stung so badly.

"I'm so sorry! I swear I didn't mean—"

I shrugged and tried to smile. "S'okay. It's true, isn't it?"

We sat there in an awkward silence and watched a couple third-graders smacking each other with their backpacks as they walked home. They were about the same age Anne and I were when we first became friends. It was hard to stay mad at someone you've known practically your whole life.

I tried to joke our way back to normal. "So, now that we both agree that I'm clueless when it comes to guys, I concede to the wisdom of the expert. What do you think the deal is with David?"

Anne squeezed my hand as a thank-you for letting her comment slide. She took a deep breath and rubbed her temples trying to channel her inner yenta. Anne took her relationship guru status seriously. "Well, first—you have similar interests. That's good. You are both passionate about your art. Also good. He's tall and has surprisingly ripped abs, which I checked out for you when he changed out of his paint shirt the other day. That's better than good. And you've been doing this whole Betterment Plan for almost two months. A plan *I* devised, I might add, so that *must* be good. Maybe he's noticed the change in you and decided now was the time?"

I tensed my legs and checked out the newly discovered, though faint, definition in my muscles. "The Betterment Plan? Shouldn't a guy be into you for a better reason than the fact that you ditched cheese sauce for a few weeks?"

"Puh-lease. Have you been watching reruns on the Family Channel again? He's a guy! They don't look deeper until you train them to."

"Sounds like a real catch."

"No offense, but who else are you going to catch in the next five weeks, Quigley? Prom will be here soon. So unless you have a hot second cousin from another school who your mom can call in as a favor—which if you did, I'd be pissed you didn't introduce us—but if not, it's time to lower the standards to something approaching a normal human being."

I loosened the laces of my shoes with a sigh. "Well, I guess David does qualify as 'something approaching a human being.'"

"That's the spirit! So you'll clear things up on Monday?"

I picked at a loose bit of tiled mosaic on the step. "Ripped abs? Really?"

"I know! Shocker, isn't it? But I had visual confirmation. He must work out at home or something. Shows you shouldn't judge the book by the cover."

"I'm not sure that's what they mean by that . . . but, okay, I guess. Monday."

"Excellent! Now, come in. I have to show you what T-Shirt got me yesterday."

I ran up the stairs behind Anne. Ms. Parisi seemed to have redone the walls in the hall. "Cool . . . it's fabric!"

Anne snorted. "I didn't even notice. SD must be in the tabloids again."

"SD?"

"Sperm Donor. That's what all those bitter old women call father figures like Mr. Unmentionable when they are online whining to each other."

I decided not to comment on how not "old" or "bitter" Ms. Parisi seemed. It was better to let Anne vent like this with me, instead of having to watch her do it when her mom was actually in the room. "Online? Your mom doesn't exactly seem like the support-group-online-chat type."

"No, she just makes a few calls and orders new men every time Pops hits the newsstands."

"OMG! Your mom does the escort thing?" I wondered why she never seemed to date. She was young and gorgeous and idolized by half the fashion world; it seemed a woman like that would have men falling all over her.

Anne laughed. "Gawd, no. Her preferred men come bearing rolls of wall coverings or antique side tables instead of diamonds and roses. Wait a sec. I guess I shouldn't talk! Like mother like daughter—I've got my own guy presenting me with décor!" Anne threw open her bedroom door. "Ta-daaaaa."

I stared at the DANGEROUS CURVES road sign Anne had hung over her bed. Not exactly Ethan Allen.

"Umm . . ." It was the nicest thing I could say.

"It's from T-Shirt! His latest acquisition. At first he was going to get me a DIP sign—luckily they came across this on their way back to town, or I might have let little Maria-the-freshman-nun have him."

"Where do you even buy such a thing?"

"Buy? *That* would be tacky. This is hard-earned, baby! It's just a little collecting habit some of the stage-crew guys have."

I could see a scuff on the reflective yellow backing of the sign. She was right. It was the real deal.

"Isn't it great?"

"Yeah. Pretty cool. But, aren't those signs sort of necessary? You know, on the road?"

"Paranoid, are we? It's not like it's a stop sign or something. Don't act all stuck up—T-Shirt saw it and thought of me. I think it's sweet. Come on, grab your notebook. Now that I got my guy, we need to work on a strategy for hooking you an Art King."

I gave a last uneasy look at the sign and followed her down to the kitchen.

• •

Chapter Six

I stood by the door and fiddled with my sketchbook.
After seeing Zander's struggle to capture his wedding couture design, I decided to make this into a working afternoon out. His apology for depicting my bustled behind about twelve sizes bigger than my head was hard to take as sincere, considering he had to wipe his eyes from laughing so hard.

After we looked through the photography exhibit, we could head to the sculpture hall and work on sketching figures. I checked the side pockets on my cargo pants to make sure I'd grabbed enough of the gray gummy eraser. Two should be enough. They felt like industrial-strength silly putty and didn't wreck the paper, even if you had to erase twenty times in one spot. I hiked my baggy pants back up. My favored slouch style was getting a little too slouch what with all of Anne's Betterment Plan harassment.

The resulting gap between my khakis and my black tee was bordering on obscene.

I was trying to decide whether I had to switch to jeans when Zander pulled up in a tiny dark green convertible. If that wasn't shocking enough, he got out wearing a crisp blue button-down shirt over fitted cream jeans. I'd gotten so used to seeing him in his clingy dark gray V-neck tees and faded jeans, I thought it was his personal uniform. His hair was different, too. A second look at the *GQ* fashion plate walking up my driveway sent me scurrying up the stairs. I had to find something else to wear and quick, or I'd look ridiculous walking in next to him.

I yanked off my trainers and ripped through the hangers in my closet. Near the back was a strapless dress Anne bought me with diagonal purple, black, and teal lines running down the body. The top was way too bare, but maybe I could put my black top back on over it. I pulled the stretchy material on and groaned. Anne being Anne had bought a vavoomy too-short style that was more "club scene" than "art museum."

At the sound of the doorbell, I grabbed my strappy black sandals and ran down the stairs. I looked ridiculous, but my parents were out and I didn't want him to think I had flaked and leave if no one answered. I began to pull my black tee on over the slinky dress as I opened the door.

"Wow," Zander said.

My head poked through the neckline. I stuck my other arm in and pulled the T-shirt smooth over the dress with a sigh. "I know. Awful, isn't it?"

"Um, no. I mean, on you, yes." His eyes widened at my gasp. "No, I didn't mean it like that. It's just not you."

Watching Zander stammer and turn red on my porch was pretty fun. "So—on someone else, this dress would be great . . . but not on me?"

Zander took a deep breath and slowly exhaled before smiling. "I'm going to shut up now."

"I just didn't know you were going to dress up. I saw you walk up and couldn't find a skirt, so grabbed this. If you just want to wait a minute, I'll go find something less idiotic to wear."

"No, wait a sec." He gestured toward my dress. "May I?"

I shrugged. "You're the expert. But someday you're really going to have to stop treating me like your personal Barbie doll."

Zander felt the material and spun me around for a better look. "Actually, I was never much into Barbie."

"Ken, then?" I don't why it came out of my mouth.

Zander raised an eyebrow. "Sure. Of course. Because everyone knows all male fashion designers are gay."

"I didn't mean it like that."

"If you say so. But you'll need to stop turning that horrible shade of red. It's clashing with the dress." Zander laughed. "*Actually*, I was going to say I didn't care for Barbie because she was disproportioned. Now, suck it in."

I stuck out my tongue at the "suck it in" remark.

Zander knelt and took the sides of the dress in both hands and gave it a sharp yank down. Under my T-shirt, the former bodice of the dress slid snugly over my hips, and the bottom of the dress-turned-skirt swirled around my ankles in a graceful arc.

"There," he motioned to the mirror. "Now *that* is you."

"Wow." I resisted the urge to twirl. "You are the master." I pulled on my shoes, grabbed my sketch pads, and followed him out to the car.

He paused at the front bushes and plucked a purple flower. "Did you know that in Hawaii, to wear a flower behind your right ear means you're free and behind your left means you're taken, but in Fiji, it's the opposite?"

"Oooh, South Pacific trivia day!" I stepped up as he

opened the passenger's-side door. "I did not know that."

"So, which is it?" He twirled the flower between his fingers.

"Well, I guess the right."

Zander stepped in and tucked the flower behind my ear with a smile. He fluffed out my hair with a happy sigh. "Excellent."

I wasn't sure if he was referring to my answer or the look he created. Something intense about his eyes caused a weird flutter in my stomach. "Of course, I didn't say whether I was a Fijian or Hawaiian."

Zander laughed and hopped into the two-seater. "Too true."

I looked around the tiny car. The leather glistened and the wood inlays gleamed. Three little wipers lined up across the windshield. Someone had a thing for cars. I wouldn't have guessed that about him. I was starting to wonder what else there was about Zander I didn't know. A metal box of chalk pastels was tucked between the seats.

"I'm so glad you brought your pastels! I thought you were going to give me a hard time about wanting to sketch at the museum. We are so on the same wavelength."

I pulled the box out to see which brand he used. Wow.

Rembrandt Soft Pastels, the good stuff. Zander plucked the little envelope off the front of the top-of-the-line set so quick I almost didn't catch my name printed in small even letters.

"Yep. Exact same wavelength," he said, and shoved the crumpled paper into his pocket. "It's eerie almost, isn't it?"

I pretended to study the neighbors' lawn gnome and wondered what it all meant.

• • • • • • • • • • • •

I gazed deep into the last of the photographs on the wall. The artist had done some sort of technique with bridge traffic that looked like all the cars had come to a screeching halt.

"Wonder what it was?" Zander asked.

"What what was?"

"It's like everything froze. Something big must have happened. Something . . . important." Zander leaned in to inspect the large print. "Doesn't it just drive you crazy not knowing what it was?"

Somehow when he discussed art, it didn't sound as ridiculous as many of the conversations going on around us. It wasn't just the words the people were using, it was almost like half the people turned British when they walked through the museum's doors. Long, drawn-out-vowels and clasped-

hands-in-church-clothes people mingled with wild gesticula-
tors wearing all black or bright flashes of clashing colors.

Sprinkled throughout the crowd were dressed-down
student types making notes. They looked so at home sitting cross-legged on the benches gazing at the works, it was
obvious they attended the attached design school. This art
program didn't quite reach the Art Institute of Chicago in
my mind's eye, but it was well respected and likely my only
shot with the way the rest of my grades seemed to be going.
I allowed myself to daydream about wandering through the
exhibit halls of the museum in Chicago as a student, feeling
like an insider.

Zander shook his head and gave up trying to dissect the
photograph's meaning. He shrugged with a grin. "Pretty
cool, anyway."

"Want to go do some sketching?"

Zander groaned.

I laughed and grabbed his hand so he couldn't escape,
dragging him through the crowded archway into the next
hall. Which is when I ran into someone I was not expecting
to see. A very familiar someone.

"Quigley?"

"David!"

David's surprised smile fell as he took in my hand still holding Zander's. I dropped it like a hot coal, which was about the stupidest thing to do because now I was caught between David's hurt expression and Zander's. My mouth was opening and closing like a fish's, but I wasn't sure what to say that wouldn't make things worse.

"Well, I'm glad you got to see the exhibit." David nodded with a tight smile and then walked fast toward the exit.

I fought the urge to run after him. There was no point. I could tell him that Zander was just a friend, but he probably wouldn't believe that anyway. I didn't owe David anything, but it hadn't even occurred to me that I'd run into him.

Zander studied me with the same intensity he had used on the photography exhibit for a long minute before shrugging and looking away with a small smile.

"I'm sorry." I had no idea why I was apologizing, but it just felt like the thing to do.

"No worries."

I motioned toward the exit. "That was just—"

"Let me guess. The pompous no-talent art hack?"

"Yes."

"I figured."

We stood in awkward silence in the narrow archway until a woman in a big fur coat brushed past me and nudged me into his chest. I didn't remember his wearing cologne in the design studio, but the light citrus scent seemed perfect for him.

"Maybe we should stand somewhere else," I said.

Zander reached down and took my hand again and swung it lightly. "Want to go sketch?"

I let him lead me to the much less busy sculpture hall. I was feeling a little too confused by his sudden interest in sketching, or maybe the fact that we seemed to be walking through a museum holding hands, to be in charge. He picked out a small room with two female bronze figures on opposite sides of the gallery. Between the two sculptures was a wide flat bench.

"Perfect! Which do you want?" he asked.

"We're not sketching the same one?"

"Not unless you want to shred the last bit of confidence I have left in me today," he said with a laugh.

"Okay. I'll take her." I pointed at the young mother figure and left the dancer to him.

"Good." Zander placed my sketchbook and the box of

pastels on one end of the bench and then sat cross-legged facing the other with a thick triangular stick of charcoal and his own pad. "Give those pastels a try for me."

"Are you sure? I brought charcoal pencils, too."

"I'm more of a steady black-and-white sort of person," he said over his shoulder. "You, on the other hand, exude all these flashes of brilliant color where you least expect them."

I smiled and picked up a dark purple. As soon as the soft chalk of the pastel smoothed over the textured paper, I felt all the confusion and stress melt away. Even when I felt Zander lean against me, back to back, it just felt warm and natural. As I added the final shadows of my figure's contours to my sketch, he finally broke the comfortable silence.

"I'm not, you know."

I leaned down and blew aside some loose chalk dust the pastels had left behind. "Not what?" I grabbed the deep blue to touch up the mother's cloak.

"You know . . . into Ken dolls."

My hand faltered and a slash of bright blue spilled onto the white background. I swallowed in an attempt to control my voice. "Oh. Good. I mean. Not good, not that there's anything—"

"Gotcha." I could hear the smile in his voice.

His hand touched my shoulder, and I looked down at his fingers holding out a gray rubbery eraser. I took it and decided I'd better keep my mouth shut before I made any further blunders that might be tougher to erase.

Chapter Seven

· ·

Anne made a rare early-morning school appearance to make up for the fact that she had been an absentee best friend the night before. The smell of floor wax was strong this early in the day, and I counted the ugly offset linoleum tiles as we walked toward our lockers. I found it easier to think things through if I distracted the frazzled surface of my brain with something else. I thought of this process as mental doodling.

"I didn't sleep at all. I really needed to talk to you last night about all of this," I said.

"I told you, T-Shirt and I were heading back and he got nailed by that lousy cop in Batville. It's a total speed trap. The road goes from fifty-five miles per hour down to fifteen in about ten feet. It's impossible *not* to speed. And then, once he stopped us, the guy went over the car to find any other violations he could possibly ticket. Car body modified too low to the ground, crack in one taillight—you wouldn't believe it. He ended up with over two hundred bucks in fines."

"Wow. Can he afford to pay that kind of ticket?"

"He'll just borrow from his dad—he gives him anything he wants. T's got the wildest plan to get back at the cop—it will be the biggest collecting expedition yet. The guy kept us so long when he was going over the car for every little thing that he added on a breaking-curfew violation since I'm still seventeen. It was totally humiliating."

"Was your mom freaked?"

"Well, it's her fault really, and I told her so." Anne glanced around to make sure we were alone. "She and Pops had to hook up at a fall fashion show—if she'd gotten knocked up in the spring runway season, I'd be eighteen by now and would never have gotten the stupid ticket."

Anne was still completely undecided on future careers, but I really thought she'd be missing her calling if she didn't go into law.

"Interesting argument."

Anne sighed. "Yeah, Mom didn't go for that one, either.

The ticket is only thirty-five bucks, but you have to have a parent or guardian show up at the station or courthouse. I think that's what got her so upset. She was going on and on about how I was risking university acceptances on stupid stunts. But I think she's just afraid someone will see her and she'll look bad."

Anne pouted. "Ever since all those celeb losers started picking her gowns for their multimillion-dollar money-pit weddings, she's had paparazzi snapping her around town, trying to get first glance at the dresses. She even had to get a police escort from the beading store once. She's paranoid if she seems remotely interesting to them as more than a top designer, someone might go digging and ta-daaa—out comes dear old dad! Now she's going to be even more all over me than she was before. It's so unfair."

"Well, at least you didn't have any new 'room décor' items in the car." I pointed out. I hadn't yet figured out how to convince her to nix supporting T-Shirt's little hobby.

"True. Anyway, that's why I didn't get your many, *many* messages until this morning. You need to fill me in on everything with Zander. I need details. How was the kiss good night?" Anne asked.

"Well, considering it was three in the afternoon, it wasn't

so much a good-night-kiss sort of moment. And the twins from down the road throwing a Frisbee that nearly took his head off didn't add to the romance of the situation."

"So—no kiss? Not even a peck?"

"Well, no," I admitted.

Anne looked at me with her head cocked. "Quigley. . . are you sure you're reading this whole situation the right way?"

"What do you mean?"

"Well, you thought you had this big moment between you—right?"

Something about her tone was causing a whole different, and much less fun, fluttering in my stomach than I'd had in the museum. I nodded and pushed open the hall door that led to our lockers.

"But then he didn't go in for the kiss good-bye. How did he leave it exactly?"

"Well, he just sort of waved and said he'd see me Wednesday." Hearing it out loud, the whole thing did sound totally lame. Could I have imagined everything? "But he paid admission and for lunch at the museum café."

"Who asked who?" Anne asked.

"I told him about the exhibit and he asked if I wanted to go with him."

"Well, whoever asks, pays. So that's not much of an indicator."

"But after the thing with David, he held my hand."

"Were you upset?"

"I guess. I felt like a complete jerk."

"So Zander's your friend. He knew you were already dealing with a bunch of guilt over insulting David last week. Doesn't it sort of make sense that he would try to comfort you?"

I was such an idiot. She was right. "But wait! What about all that Ken-doll stuff? Why would he have made such a point to tell me he's straight?"

"Oh my God, Quigley. You basically told a straight guy you thought he was gay. You're lucky he's mature and so laid back or he might have peeled off in his hot little convertible and left you in the dust. He's your *friend*. Which way you swing is a pretty big part of your life, don't you think? I think that would be a misconception he'd want to clear up just so you could get to know him better . . . as friends."

My ears were on fire. My face was probably solid red. Anne gave me a little sympathy hug as we neared our lockers.

"Look. I'm not saying all this to make you feel dumb. It's just that I've been in a lot more of these situations than you have. I don't want you to get hurt or disappointed. And I also don't want you to miss out on *something* with David because you're chasing after *nothing* with Zander."

My laugh came out bitter. "David? I'm sorry, were you not following the story? If he didn't hate me before, he does now. I doubt he'll ever speak to me again."

Anne laughed and pointed to my locker. "Don't be so sure."

I stared at the single flower stuck through the handle of my locker. A little tag hanging from the stem was signed with "Love" and an unmistakable David drawing of a crown.

"I don't get it." It was the understatement of the year.

Anne rubbed her hands together and giggled. "All these years I've been trying to teach you the ways of the master— you must have picked up something!"

"But—"

"Didn't I tell you? Keep several on the line—it's the only way to go. I wouldn't let on to David that you and Zander are only friends. Let's just see how far you can play up the aftereffects of your pseudo-date."

"I guess so. Thanks."

Pseudo-date. Any excitement from getting my first-ever flower from a guy was flattened by the realization of how wrong I had read things with Zander. I was hopeless at all this love stuff. At least Anne had saved me from making an idiot out of myself on Wednesday night.

She gave a little wave and ran off toward the theater to track down T-Shirt.

I put the flower up to my nose and sniffed. It smelled like dye, probably from the unnatural pink-red on the petals. Was I supposed to carry this around with me all day? I didn't know the etiquette. I hung up my jacket and pulled out my hated chem textbook. At the last minute, I tucked the flower up on the shelf and slammed the metal door shut, hoping it wouldn't die before I got it home.

I headed toward the science lab thinking about Anne's take on recent events. It all made perfect sense. Not that I much liked the perfect sense it made.

"Earth to Quigley," David said.

"David! I didn't see you."

"I know. I've been chasing you for the last ten minutes."

"I'm so sorry."

David smiled his crooked smile, which was a hundred times nicer than the cocky Art King smirk. "S'okay. You didn't even see me."

I picked at the frayed edge of my chem cover. "No. I mean, sorry about everything. At the museum—" I decided not to bring up the barrage of insults I sent his way in the cafeteria. Maybe he'd forgotten.

"It's okay. Us 'pompous jerks' can handle a few blows to the ego."

Okay, maybe not. At least he was smiling about it.

"But seriously," David went on, "I was the one who told you to go. I'm just glad you didn't miss it. What did you think about those different speed techniques?"

"They were pretty cool. I really liked the ones where it was like everything sped up and then froze."

"Right! The ones on the far wall after you come in?" he asked.

"Yes! The big square ones. How did they do that?"

"I think it's sort of like what Mrs. Albertt was talking about. Hey, maybe we can sign out some cameras after school and go to a park and try that out?"

David opened the door to the chem lab for me. I gave up. Boys officially confused the bejeebees out of me.

"Sure. That sounds good," I said.

"Great. It's a date!"

I was glad the door had shut behind me before he could see my shocked face. I had also completely forgotten to thank him for the flower.

· · · · · · · · · · · ·

At 3:05, I waited for David by my locker and tried to calm my nerves. It was weird. I'd known him for three and a half years, but his new, mellow, sheepish side made him seem like a complete stranger. I was going on a date with a complete stranger. I had every right to be nervous, going on a date with a complete stranger. I tried to think of how many other ways I could fit "going on a date" into a sentence, aiming for twenty-two, give or take.

It wasn't like I never went out. But there was something sort of cool about coming to class one Monday morning, expecting to go home and do homework after school and, instead, ending up going on a date. Maybe this is what it felt like to be Anne. She could go on three dates every afternoon, if she felt like it.

Today, she was actually going on her own date to some mysterious locale to do some mysterious thing that she couldn't talk about during lunch. Though when T-Shirt looked down to wipe some mustard off his DOESN'T PLAY WELL WITH OTHERS top, she mouthed, "Tell you later," before he caught her. So I wouldn't be in suspense for too long.

Unfortunately, I couldn't get any last-minute advice from

her. Two minutes after I sat down to enjoy my banana and yogurt with granola, David plunked his tray down and slid into the seat next to me. He sat sprawled out, eating his burger one-handed with the other arm draped casually across the back of my chair. I couldn't figure the guy out, but I couldn't resist feeling the tiniest bit smug when I saw the death glare coming from "Maria," the unnamed freshman, at the next table.

I glanced at my watch, again—3:10. I had to get my head back in the game. After all, any minute I'd be going on a date. I pushed away the twinge of disappointment my date wasn't with Zander, but Anne was probably right. A couple of little shrieking neighbor kids might not make for the ideal romantic background, but it shouldn't have been a complete deal breaker for your basic postdate kiss. I had obviously misread the situation and had to accept that. No sense in throwing something away over nothing. With prom only a month away and no other prospects in sight, David's sudden change of heart should be welcomed.

I wished I'd worn something cuter. But what was a girl to do when she had no clue while getting ready for school that she'd end up going on a date?

The hall door opened. David juggled two cameras and a handful of film cartridges. I rushed to help him before he dropped a lens, which would be a very unromantic thing to happen right as we were going on a date.

Chapter Eight

• •

"I can't wait to see what I got," David said. "That's the only drag about print instead of digital. At least with digital it's all right there."

I cringed as my malt made a giant *slurp*. "I can get access to the developing lab on Thursday."

"You think I caught that squirrel as he jumped? I heard the click at the right time, but I have trouble with all the calculations involved in shutter speeds."

"Me, too. I'm terrible with math. And a lot of other subjects." I laughed and shifted my legs. We were sitting on the hood of David's car, which was still hot from the engine.

"So, where are you going to school next year?" David asked, waving to a group of jocks who parked next to us. They didn't go to our school, but looked familiar from around town.

"I'm not sure. I'm keeping my options open." It wasn't exactly a lie. They were wide open.

"Pretty late in the game to still be choosing."

"What can I say? I'm a picky girl." I slid off the hood to throw away my cup. I hoped when I got back he'd have dropped the subject.

"So who are your front runners?" David called after me.

So much for dropping the subject. I decided to go with a dash of honesty to round out my evasiveness. "Well, of course, the Art Institute of Chicago would be my top pick—"

"Oh yeah. I got in there, too."

I stared at him. "You got into the Art Institute of Chicago?"

"Sure. They dug my sculptures—remember that one I won citywide with last year? Sent a slide of that and four others from the same series for my portfolio submission. But I'm going with Michigan State instead—go Spartans!"

David had gotten accepted by the Art Institute of Chicago. And he was turning them down. I touched my temples where a steady, rapid pulse beat in time with my heart.

"Hey, you okay? You look kind of funny," he said.

"Brain freeze," I lied.

"Oh, I hate that!"

I tried to make my voice steady. Maybe I had misunderstood. "So, wait. You were accepted, like officially offered a place, at the *Art Institute.* And you turned it down?"

"Yeah. There's no money in art. Unless you want to be one of those computer graphics techie freaks—and I'm hardly the living-in-my-mother's-basement-spending-twenty-hours-a-day-on-the-computer type." He flicked a piece of ice back at his friends as they hopped in and cranked the bass. "Besides, Michigan's topped the best-party-school list for the last three years running. I'll be stylin' in that Spartan red. College is all about the experience, right? I figure I'll go into business or something. I can always be the Art King in my free time."

I watched David walk to the trash to throw out his sundae cup. So all the years of our competition were about the competition, and not the art? Apparently, I was going on a date with not only a complete stranger, but a complete idiot.

"So, Quigley—got any plans for Friday? I was thinking me, you, Anne, and T could go catch that new Keith Gordon flick."

"Yeah, well, Anne's not exactly his biggest fan, so I doubt that will happen."

I tried to cover my gasp. Stunned by the idea of David

passing on the Art Institute, it was the closest I'd come to spilling the truth about Anne's father in nine years.

David looked at me strangely. "Who doesn't like Keith Gordon? I thought every living breathing female was into him. I thought I was being thoughtful, giving you guys a little eye candy while we watch things blow up."

I fought the urge to gag. The idea of Anne's biological father being eye candy was beyond gross. I'd known about their relationship so long that it was hard to see him as a sex symbol. He was just my friend's deadbeat dad. Ewww.

David was waiting for an explanation.

"I'm not sure. She just thinks he's full of himself."

"Keith Gordon? He runs around the world doing charity work for the poor and donates his free time in the States to environmental causes." David laughed at the idea. "Sorry, but Anne's nuts."

Time to wrap this up, or I'd put my foot into it. "Look, I need to get home." I looked at my watch. "I've got a big trig test tomorrow."

"Okay. I'll drive you."

The typical David cocky attitude was dropping as the blocks passed in silence. He was the Dr. Jekyll and Mr. Hyde of potential prom dates, though his magic potion came in the form of being in the presence of other people. It was a shame they weren't holding prom on a deserted island, or this might actually work. I reached for the door handle as he pulled into my driveway.

He touched my arm. "Quigley, hold up a second, okay? Look, I'm not sure how I screwed things up, but it kind of feels like I did somehow. I shouldn't have said your friend was nuts. Anne's cool. And so are you."

I wasn't sure what to say. I let my hand slip off the door handle.

Encouraged, David rushed on. "It's just— Well, I get nervous when I like somebody, and then I say stupid things. And you make me nervous. I know I sound like a dork saying that. But could you maybe cut me some slack at first, and I'll try not to be such an idiot next time?"

The crooked smile was back. It was a hard smile to resist.

"Yeah. Okay, I guess." I smiled, too. So there was going to be a next time. I'd have to think about how I felt about that. Once my head stopped reeling from his college admission, well, admission.

"Thanks."

I thought he was leaning in for a hug. Which is why I

was shocked to find myself with the stick shift digging into my side, eyes wide open and staring at the space between his eyebrows, while getting thoroughly and unmistakably kissed.

· · · · · · · · · · · ·

I sat in Anne's living room waiting for her to get home. Ms. Parisi brought me a glass of iced white tangerine tea with a large flat spoon filled with honey. A sprig of mint floated in the pale brown drink. It was like being in a restaurant or something. I wasn't quite sure what to do with the spoon after I drizzled it into the glass, so I sucked off the excess honey to avoid leaving a sticky spot on the table. I watched the honey clump into little balls as it hit the ice cubes and sank to the bottom.

"She should be home any time now," she said. She sat down in the armchair opposite me and folded her hands in her lap, then leaned forward and smiled. "So what's going on these days with you, Quigley?"

Ms. Parisi had a way of asking questions like she actually wanted to know the answer. It wasn't something you saw too often in grown-ups. It seemed rude to spit out the usual auto reply "School's good; Mom and Dad started collecting books for the kids' charity book drive; I'm looking forward to the summer" stuff.

I set my glass of tea down. "I just got kissed and I'm not quite sure how I feel about that."

I don't know which of us was more surprised by my statement. I turned bright red, and Ms. Parisi's tinkle of laughter echoed up into the exposed beams of the two-story-high ceiling. It wasn't mean laughter, though, and she hopped up and gave me a hug before nestling down on the sofa next to me.

"So tell me all about this boy. Oh wait—was it Zander?"

"I wish." It popped out of my mouth before my brain even registered the thought. Where did that come from? No sense in going there. If a guy wasn't into you, he wasn't into you. And if anyone was an expert on guys being into you, it would be Anne.

Ms. Parisi patted my hand. "I'm sorry. I shouldn't have asked. I just thought I sensed a connection between you." She lowered her voice and grinned. "So who was this masked kisser?"

"His name is David. He's completely full of himself and cocky and has this amazing talent for art that he doesn't even appreciate—"

"Hmm. Doesn't sound like your type."

"Well, I haven't exactly had enough boyfriends to have a type," I said. "And Anne thought he was okay."

Ms. Parisi sighed. "Sometimes, even best friends don't really know what's best for us. Anne's seeing things from her perspective. She likes those momentary thrills, the excitement and the roller-coaster life. I don't know this boy, but I've known you for a long time. What's good for Anne might not be the best fit for you."

"I guess. But it's weird. I can't figure him out. Right before he kissed me, I just wanted to be done with him. But then he gave this whole speech about how he says dumb stuff when he gets nervous or uncomfortable—which I can totally relate to." The memory of my stupid Ken-doll remark make my cheeks go hot. "I just know I'd want a second chance if I said something jerky. Besides, he gave me one for saying some really mean stuff about him last week. But then he went and laid one on me! So now, I don't know if I'm thinking I might like him because of what he said or just because of the kiss."

"That *is* confusing."

"And even though I feel like I might like him, I sort of hate him, too. He got into my dream college and he's turning it down! Who does that?"

"Which was your top choice?"

"It's silly because it's such a long shot. But it would be beyond amazing to get into the Art Institute of Chicago."

"Great school," Ms. Parisi said. "Have you ever been to visit?"

"No. But I've memorized every word on the Web site and have the real-time satellite pictures of Chicago up as my screen saver. The city looks so great with that long green park along the water and all those trees here and there, right in the middle of the concrete-and-steel jungle. Did you know they turn the river green for St. Patrick's Day? Even the dorm rooms are in big skyscrapers. Can you imagine being in a building filled with other artists. How cool would that be?"

"Chicago is a great town. I've done many shows there," Ms. Parisi said. "I could see you fitting in well there. Solid Midwest values combined with the arts and culture of a big city."

"I guess I'll take your word for it. It would be pretty hard to talk my parents into a trip across the country to visit a place that hasn't even accepted me."

"Did you send a portfolio?"

I took a long swig of tea to help stop any tears of embarrassment. "Yes. It was returned with a 'no distinct style, consistency' comment. They said I could resubmit later in the year if my 'focus matured' for a chance at one of the cancellation spots. But it seems so impossible. I guess I should thank David for passing on the offer—maybe I'll end up getting his spot."

Ms. Parisi sighed. "Anne's latest choice is Yale."

"Wow. It must be great to have a daughter who's so smart she can go anywhere. You must be so proud."

"Well, if I didn't suspect that the school's famous Sex Week was at the bottom of this university-of-the-month kick, I'd probably feel better." Ms. Parisi laughed.

I couldn't help but laugh with her. That would be so Anne.

"I'm sure she'll be fine wherever she goes. She's just one of those people who things always turn out right for," I said.

"I hope you're right. Speak of the devil—"

Anne slammed the front door behind her and ran halfway up the stairs before she saw me. She was wearing baggy camo pants, and her black T-shirt was tied in a knot to reveal her midriff. The olive-green slogan THEY CAN SEND ME TO COLLEGE—BUT THEY CAN'T MAKE ME THINK! stood out as she leaned over the banister, "Hey, Quigley. Come on up!" Her military boots clomped up the Oriental stair runner and disappeared.

Ms. Parisi shook her head and gave me another hug. "Go ahead on up. Thanks for the talk. It's nice to feel needed."

"It's nice to feel listened to." Her wistful look as she glanced up at the empty stairwell was hard to watch. "You know, I would never have a talk like this with my own mom."

"No?" Her voice lilted up on a note of hope.

I swung my backpack over one shoulder and smiled. "Nope." I ran up the stairs to Anne's room without looking back. I was pretty sure Ms. Parisi would be smiling.

I jerked back from the blast of music as I opened Anne's door.

"Why is it so loud!" I screamed.

Anne rushed over and pulled me in before slamming the door and locking it. She had taken the speakers off their shelves and aimed them at the door. I tripped over the wires and caught up with her in the much quieter window seat at the far end of her room.

"You would not believe what just happened to me," she said.

"*You* would not believe what just happened to *me!*" I said.

She leaned back and assessed my odds of topping her.

"Nice shirt, by the way."

"It's T's."

"I assumed. His pants, too?"

"How'd you guess?"

"Maybe I don't want to hear the story of what just happened to you."

She smacked my arm. "Nothing like that! I went on a collecting expedition!"

I groaned. "Anne! What are you thinking? You'll be toast if you get caught taking those things."

"I know! I'm not stupid."

I tried to figure out how many of our conversations included her saying that exact phrase. Maybe T should get that printed on a shirt for her.

"See, today we didn't take anything. It was more of a reconnaissance mission. Remember that jerk of a cop from Batville?"

"The one who gave you a ticket for breaking curfew?"

"Only because he took so long writing the other tickets, but yes. T-Shirt decided to get even with him."

"Your boyfriend decides to take revenge on a police officer?! That's bound to end up well."

The "but they can't make me think" part of her shirt appeared all too appropriate.

"That cop's been busting people for trumped-up speeding charges and made-up vehicle violations for a long time. It's not fair. Besides, they're not going to do anything bad to the guy, just embarrass him a little. And T-Shirt's not my *boyfriend*. I don't believe in that term. Unless it is used in the plural."

"Yeah, yeah. So what did you do?"

"Oh my gosh, it was so exciting. I swear, my heart was about to fly right through my chest. We went down to the police station—"

My stomach flipped. "Anne, are you insane?"

"No, wait. This was brilliant. We all drove down there and waited for the cop to pull in. It's that tiny concrete building next to the DQ, so we sat eating Blizzards on the outside benches, real nonchalant. After he pulls in and goes inside, T knew he'd be signing his radio and equipment in, filling out logs and so forth, for at least fifteen to twenty minutes."

I would have commented on the fact that her new non-boyfriend seemed surprisingly well acquainted with the goings-on inside a police station. But I was having a hard enough time just breathing.

"So the cop goes inside and I walk over to the parking lot

like I want to throw away my cup and can't find a trash can.
But I cross on the far side of the police car and, real smooth,
take this out of my pocket."

Sure she was gonna pull out something crazy like a pocket
knife, I just stared at the small piece of broken ruler. She
grinned.

"I don't get it."

She rolled her eyes in exasperation. "I measured the
bolts."

"You measured the bolts?"

"In the light bar. Batville still has those old-style cop cars
with the thing bolted on top of the roof that holds all the
lights and sirens and stuff."

"And you measured the bolts . . . for what reason?"

"For T-Shirt and those guys. Now they know what
wrenches to bring with them when they take it off for the
collection. It should save them a bunch of time. *Critical*
time."

I forced myself to watch Anne's ceiling fan blade circle ten
times before I thought I could speak in a somewhat normal
tone. Maybe I should have gone for fifteen.

"But what if someone saw you? I can't believe T-Shirt

would ask you to do that! What a jerk. Don't you get it? Not only are they bringing you down with them, but when it all goes bad, you're going to end up the one arrested or something—"

"Arrested for what? Assault with a deadly ruler?" Anne laughed and flipped the broken ruler onto her bedspread.

"It's not funny," I said.

"Well, it kind of is. I'm not going to be with them when they do it, *Mom*, so even if they get caught, I won't. They did it this way so it didn't look like they thought about it ahead of time. If they get caught, T-Shirt's going to say he recognized the cop and lost it when he thought about all the tickets and exaggerated charges. They figure the guy won't make trouble and expose himself for harassing drivers. Even if he does, it looks better if it was a spur-of-the-moment thing than if they had planned it."

There's always a point with Anne where arguing any more is senseless and liable to make her dig her heels in and push it even further. One look at her father's trademark perfect-but-rigid jawline and her arms folded across her chest, and I knew we were there. I shrugged in defeat and scratched at the old paint stain on my jeans leg. It was enough to appease her.

"Look. I know you disapprove of T-Shirt and his extra-curricular activities. But it's cool, okay?"

"Sure."

We sat in awkward silence. I considered leaving.

"Change of subject? Please?" Anne asked.

I sat straight up. I was so worried about Anne's latest insanity, I'd completely forgotten about David.

"David kissed me!" I blurted out for the second time in an hour. I hoped it wasn't some new smooch-specific sort of Tourette's syndrome. It could be awkward in church or during cultural affairs lectures.

"David kissed you!" she yelled. "Wait. How did I not know this?"

"Well, I barely knew it myself. It was out of the blue. We went to the park and tried some different F-stop speeds and intentionally blurred effects like the ones I saw in the large pieces at the mu—"

"Artsy-smartsy, blah-blah-blah—just get to the good stuff!"

I laughed. It was rare to elicit this sort of reaction from Anne. It wasn't often my wild-child friend wanted to live vicariously through me.

"So he was saying that he says dumb things when he likes

someone and that he likes me, so was saying a lot of them."

"Excellent! You have so much in common."

I threw a pillow at her.

"So then he leaned in and I thought, 'Oh, right—hug,' so I leaned in, and then all of a sudden he was kissing me!"

"Excellent! Just excellent. Was it a good kiss?"

"What do I know? It was a kiss. I was sort of too shocked to analyze the goodness of it."

"Understood." Anne nodded her head with a goofy smile. "You know what this means, don't you?"

"No! I don't. That's why I came right over here. I don't have a clue what this means or if this is a good thing or what."

"Well, some of that remains to be seen. But the important thing is . . . we can double for prom!"

I thought about David's Keith Gordon movie-night suggestion. I debated bringing it up, but with the close call on a blow-out fight over the collection expeditions, it didn't seem like a good idea to admit how close I'd come to slipping up. Maybe another time Anne would think it was funny.

"I thought you were weeks away from making that decision," I said.

"Well, sure. But if you're with David, I'll just go with

T-Shirt. It'll be way more fun if we all know each other. I'm not sure they'd let The Spikester into a school function, anyway."

"Well, I don't know if David's going to ask me."

"I'll tell T to make sure he does, and quick—none of this screwing-around-leaving-a-girl-in-suspense stuff."

"Anne, wait. I'm not sure if I even really like David."

"Didn't you voluntarily go out with him?"

"Yes."

"Didn't you have a decent time?"

I thought back to the fun of the shoot. "I guess."

"Didn't you voluntarily kiss him afterward?" she asked.

"Well, actually no. Not entirely."

"Doesn't matter. Point is, you didn't hate it. See? *That* is a real date—none of this who-paid, who-looked-at-who-for-longest or touched-whose-hand nonsense. When you're on a date, you know you're on a date."

"I guess."

"Besides, you guys have all that art stuff in common. And the best part is that he's practically best friends with T-Shirt."

I wasn't sure the last bit was the best endorsement.

"So, done deal. He'll ask. You'll say yes. We'll get some

cool ride and have a blast!" Anne grabbed her *Teen Vogue* and flipped through the formal section.

Her "cool ride" comment brought an involuntary flashback of a tiny MGB roadster. T-Shirt would probably opt for something more along the lines of an obnoxious Hummer limo. "I guess."

She held the magazine down and *tsk tsk*'ed as she carefully ripped out several pages. She crumpled them into a ball and launched them toward her wastebasket. One of the pages bounced off the rim, and I could see the Victoria Parisi logo on the bottom corner.

"This is so great. We should start looking at dresses tomorrow. Crap, we have Mom's design thing tomorrow night. Thursday, then—after school?"

My head was nodding as it spun from the day's events. I gathered my books off Anne's bed and caught sight of the ruler. I hoped she knew what she was doing.

Ms. Parisi's voice barely registered over the still-blaring music. "Anne—I'm going now. Linguini with clams is on its way from Viviano's. There's a twenty pinned to the board by the phone. Quigley, do you need a ride home? I can drop you on my way."

I looked back down at the ruler. Despite our earlier talk,

the idea of being in the small car with Anne's mom now seemed less than enticing.

"No, thank you, Ms. Parisi. I'm going to walk down to the bus."

Anne nodded. "BP, baby! Way to stay with the program."

I decided not to comment on my motivation for hoofing it.

"Okay, hon'. See you tomorrow night!" Ms. Parisi called.

I waited until I heard the garage close to let Anne lead me down to the front door.

Chapter Nine

• •

I watched Zander's dark brows wrinkle as he pulled the pencil along the paper in little jags. What should have been the smooth line of my high-waisted skirt looked more like he'd done the drawing on an Etch A Sketch.

I really had to thank Anne for saving me from looking like an idiot for expecting Zander to be interested in more than friendship and drawing lessons. His mood was all business since I walked in. Not a flirt in sight.

"You don't have to press so hard," I said. "Loosen up and the line will come out smoother."

"What—" he asked. "You don't like the scraggly look?"

"Well, if you wanted to use that long, shaggy mohair fabric from last week, you'd be all set. Though it might be a drag to wear to a summer garden party."

I watched The Spikester from across the room. He'd taken the garden party theme to a new level and was carefully poking flowers through the strategically located holes in Anne's fishnet sheath. The skimpy white bikini she was wearing slowly disappeared under the brightly colored petals. He used small purple and yellow flowers to make one line across her hip curl up and over her clearly visible belly button.

It was an impressive design, and I pulled my sketchbook out. It would be even better if I could capture Ms. Parisi at her desk in the background, staring at the pair and taking such frequent sips from her tightly gripped coffee mug that I began to wonder if it was really coffee, or something a little stronger.

"Are you cheating on me?" Zander asked.

Anne's ears were set to instinctively tune in to that phrase, and I heard her little gasp. I stared hard at the page and tried to think of how to answer. His accusation came out of nowhere. Did one ice cream and an unexpected kiss constitute cheating? And cheating on what? Didn't you have to be involved with someone before you could be cheating on him? No wonder his mood had been so brusque. It happened only yesterday—how did he even know, anyway?

I allowed myself a millisecond to gloat that I was right in thinking our museum moment had meant something and that Anne, the mistress of love, was wrong . . . and then quickly bowed to her experience in such matters and adopted her tactic of talking her way out of a mess by going on the offensive.

"*Cheating* is a little harsh, isn't it?" I asked, with one hand on my hip.

Zander raised one eyebrow. "Well, I have caught you red-handed all wrapped up in the designs of another man." He pointed down to the row of little flowers crawling up the sketchbook.

"Oh. That." I dropped my hand and tried to ignore eavesdropping Anne's snicker.

"No, no. Go back to that whole indignant look," he said. "It works with the dress. Very Daughters-of-the-American-Revolution haughty. I like it."

"Thanks." I reached over with a smile to swipe his pencil and sketched a few wispy background figures sipping tea and wearing large hats onto his page. Satisfied I had redeemed myself, or at least distracted him from talk of cheating, I returned his charcoal pencil. His hand made light graceful strokes across the paper. "Hey, you're doing much better!"

Zander nodded. "Maybe that's what I've been missing. I need to place my dresses in a scene to get a feel for what I'm drawing. When I think about just the dress, I get flustered."

"I know what you mean. You just have to make sure that the background slides right off the eye so that the dress is the main focus. Kind of like in those photos we saw at the mus—" I stopped short as my thoughts flew back to my afternoon with David.

"So, speaking of—did you run into that David guy at school? I hope he wasn't too upset." Zander had a cute habit of reading my mind.

"Upset?" I made an effort to make my voice rise with innocence, though it came out more of a squeak.

"Well, sure. Kind of a blow for a guy to see a girl he likes on a date with some other guy."

"Right. True. That wouldn't be a good thing." So it was a date. I could kill Anne. Thanks to her convincing me Zander wasn't interested, within one week I'd managed go from having no prospects of the boy persuasion, to cheating on not one guy but two.

"Are you okay?" Zander asked.

"I'm just not feeling so great."

Zander jumped up. "Here, take my stool." He rifled through his satchel and pulled out a bottle of water. "Drink."

I sipped his water and stared at my bare feet. I'd just have to explain to David that we were better off as friends. It's not like they would ever meet each other again. Zander's hands were warm on my shoulders as he gave them a little rub through the thin silk of the blouse. I could get used to this treatment.

"Feel better?" he asked. "It isn't the dress, is it? I thought I used your original measurements, but it's a pretty fitted style right over the ribs." He pinched the back seam of the dress. "Hey. Not too tight at all—looks loose by at least a half inch. You haven't been losing weight on me, have you?"

"I don't think so," I stammered. Hanging out with a guy whose business it was to know your measurements was a little strange.

"Hmm. Maybe I measured wrong. This is definitely too loose. Good Daughters of the American Revolution shouldn't be able to slouch so comfortably in their garden-party frocks."

I managed a weak laugh.

"But seriously, are you okay? I could give you a lift home if you want to call it a night."

Ms. Parisi's heels clicked toward us. "Are you not feeling well, Quigley?" she asked.

"Probably too many carrots, or something," I mumbled.

The Spikester was taking advantage of Ms. Parisi's

distraction to start a playful game of "he loves me, he loves me not" with Anne's dress.

"I offered to give her a ride, Ms. Parisi," Zander said.

"That sounds like a good idea. We only have another half hour here anyway. Why don't you head home and get some rest."

Guilt slid over me, but a half hour to spend with Zander, now that I knew he was into me, was too tempting to pass up. "Okay. If you're sure."

A giggling Anne flashed me the universal "Call me!" sign with one hand as The Spikester rushed to pick up the little pile of petals from the floor before Ms. Parisi noticed.

· · · · · · · · · · · ·

Zander rushed to the passenger side and opened my door before I could.

"Why, thank you, kind sir," I said in my best Southern-belle drawl.

"Feeling better?" he asked.

"I am. I think I just needed some fresh air."

"Well, you've come to the right place then," he said as he unlatched the top of the little convertible and folded it back.

"There we go." He snapped the last edge of the leather cover down.

"This is such a great car."

"She's my baby. She was pretty rough when I bought her, but I got a few books and, piece by piece, brought her back to life. Can you believe I only paid four hundred dollars for her?"

"No way."

"Well, that was without an engine, transmission, spark plugs, and one of the tires was shot. Not to mention someone thought spray paint was the way to cover up her rust spots."

"So you weren't in the get-a-new-car-for-the-ol'-sixteenth-birthday crowd, huh?" I hoped my attempts to find out more of his background were subtle.

"Are you?" he asked, ignoring my question.

I snorted. "Hardly. Any extra fundage in my section of the Johnson family pocketbook would be marked for college. Scholarships aren't exactly stacking up. But then again, neither are admission invitations. So maybe the universe really *does* always balance."

He chuckled. "School's definitely pricey—especially when you're not prepared."

"Well, you seem too 'Boy Scout' to not be prepared. I bet you had scholarships lined up from sophomore year."

"Freshman, actually. And I think that's the Girl Scouts who are always prepared."

I bit my tongue as another dumb Boy Scout–Girl Scout joke threatened to roll out, not wanting an accidental replay of the Barbie–Ken doll moment.

A flash of sadness or regret crossed his face, quickly shrugged away as he tugged his seat belt for the second time and glanced down at mine. Pathetic how much his little show of concern warmed me.

"I had things lined up, but things change. Life, right? What can you do? Anyway, once you decide which school will be graced by your presence, I'll give you a hand finding resources for last-minute grants. There's money still out there; tracking it down just depends on what state you'll be heading to."

The state I was heading to was one of being both touched by his offer and weirdly hurt that he could mentally pack me off to some far-flung school so nonchalantly.

We pulled out of the parking lot and headed for the freeway.

"Do you mind if we take the local roads back?" he asked.

"Not at all."

I smiled as we blew by the entrance ramp. Make that forty minutes alone with Zander. Wisps of my hair tickled my cheeks as a warm spring breeze flowed through the open car. Zander turned up the radio as an old Fleetwood Mac song started playing.

"You have a pretty voice," Zander said.

My face went hot. I didn't even realize I was singing along. He smiled and started singing, too.

"You know who has a really amazing voice?"

"Who's that?"

"Anne. She totally hides it, but it's amazing when you catch her."

"I wouldn't have guessed that. Does she get that from Ms. Parisi?"

I laughed, thinking about Ms. Parisi's tortured attempt at the "Happy Birthday" song at Anne's last party. "No, not at all."

"Good. It would be criminal for so much talent to end up in one person." Zander reached over and hit the right blinker. "Hey, can I take you somewhere? I'd love to show you this one spot, but it's totally cheesy. You have to promise not to laugh."

"I won't laugh."

He laughed. "Sure you will, but that's okay. It's too nice of a night to pass this up. That first warm breeze of spring always makes me feel this sense of hope, sort of excited and anticipating new, good things. Maybe kind of appropriate?"

He pulled off onto a windy road and slid his hand over mine. I had no idea where we were heading, but I was glad it was dark so he couldn't see my idiotic, goofy grin. I can't believe I ever thought I liked David. We were driving uphill, but it was hard to tell exactly where we were. Then, all of a sudden the trees opened up, and we were looking out on the lights of the city. I couldn't help it. I laughed.

Zander groaned. "You promised!"

"You brought me to a make-out spot," I said.

"No. I brought you to a beautiful panoramic view of the city."

"Then what are all the people in those cars doing?" I pointed at three cars discreetly spaced out in the open hilltop field.

"Okay, so I brought you to a beautiful panoramic view of the city where some people choose to park and make out."

I giggled.

"Oh yeah? Good luck getting a kiss out of me now, laughing girl."

This only made me laugh harder.

"Please stop. You're killing my mojo."

"*Mojo?* You got mojo?"

"Oh, I got mojo," he said.

I took a deep breath to stop my giggles.

"All better now?" he asked. "Now may I please show you why I brought you up here?"

"Oh, my!" I feigned shock.

Zander leaned forward and lightly banged his head against the steering wheel.

"Okay, okay. I'll stop now," I said.

He turned his head, still resting on the wheel, and studied me.

I tried to look contrite. "Seriously. Please show me why you brought me here."

"Okay. To get the full effect, I have to make a brief adjustment. Remember, open mind . . . and no giggling."

"Okay."

I held my breath as Zander leaned across me, chuckling. I smelled the same light, clean scent from the museum as he came in close to crank something on the far side of my seat. As my seat reclined inch by inch and I felt his breath on my neck, the urge to giggle left me entirely.

"There. Now me." He cranked his seat until we were both lying back staring up at the sky. "Another hobby of mine."

"Parking with girls?"

"Sure. That and the whole science of astronomy."

"Really?"

"Do you know any of the stars?"

I pointed at the three-starred belt of Orion. "I can always pick out Orion. But that's about it. I can usually see the one Dipper but I never know if it's the little one or the big one."

"I love the myths behind the constellations. I think it's so cool that different cultures have different stories for the same stars. It sort of shows what's important to them."

"Like what? Example, please."

"Well, take your Orion. He's Orion to the Greeks, but the Lakota people think of the bottom half of him as their Constellation of the Hand."

I snuggled back into the seat and breathed in the soft leather.

Zander reached over and took my hand. I shivered as he lightly traced a line across my wrist. "See? This is Orion's Belt." He trailed his fingertip up my pinky. "This is a star called Beta Eridani, from another constellation called Eridanis." His finger slid back down my pinky coming up my index finger and lightly tapped the tip. "That bright one there is Rigel." His finger came back down and rested on my thumb. "And this is the Orion Nebula, or the brightest one in Orion."

He pulled my hand close, and I felt his warm lips graze my palm before resting his arm between us, still holding my hand. Beta Eridani, Eridanis, Rigel, Orion Nebula . . . I didn't think I would ever forget those names now. If only I had studied in a setting like this, Anne would have had some serious competition at school.

"The Lakota people think the constellation represents a great chief who was very selfish. The gods made the Thunder People rip out his arm to teach him a lesson. His daughter offered to marry anyone who could return her father's arm. Fallen Star, a young warrior whose father was a star and mother was human returned the arm and married the girl, symbolizing unity between the gods and humans. You know, with a little help from a couple of kids in love."

"That's so romantic."

Zander laughed out loud and squeezed my hand.

"Sure. Some guys might use lines. But for me, talk of dismemberment always gets the girl."

"Such a player you are."

"Indeed."

"So what's the Greek version?"

"Hmm. Now that I'm thinking it through, neither of these stories seems particularly appropriate for the situation."

"Well, you already started. Can't leave a girl hanging."

Zander sighed.

"Well, there was this poor shepherd. A couple of guys came over and he didn't want to be rude to his guests, so he killed his only animal, an ox, to feed them. He didn't know it, but the guys were really gods, and they rewarded his generosity by offering him anything he wanted. What he wanted most was a son. So they told him to take the hide from the ox and bury it. And every day for the next nine months, he should go out and, well . . . urinate on it—"

"Ewww!"

Zander sat up. "See? I told you!"

"No, no. Go on," I said.

"So anyway, a boy was born in that spot—"

"So much for boys being made from frogs and snails and puppy-dog tails."

Zander laughed. "I suppose at this point in the story, you'll tell me you're an animal-rights activist and vegetarian."

"Well, I do love animals. But I also love bacon cheeseburgers, so you're probably safe."

"So the kid was this awesome hunter."

"Thus the bow . . ."

"Thus the bow. He was so good, the king hired him to kill all the beasts on his islands. And he kind of got too into the animal slaying and announced he would kill all the animals in the world."

"Uh-oh."

"Yep. Didn't go over so well with the goddess of the animals, so she sent a giant scorpion to sting him to death. Giant scorpions trump swords and strength, so Orion made a run for it. And there he is, running today." Zander lifted my hand, pointing at Orion, and then shifted to the right a bit. "And come summer, there's where the scorpion will appear in his place, still chasing him."

"That's so cool," I said, wondering what summer would bring and hoping that Zander was more "Fallen Star" than "Orion."

"You, my dear, are easily entertained."

"So what *don't* you know?" I asked.

We cranked our seats back to upright. I considered faking trouble with my twisty-knob thing to smell his cologne again, but I didn't want to seem desperate.

"Hmm. Well, I don't know how to draw very well, though

I am diligently working on that with the help of a very talented tutor. And I also don't know how to ask this without making the last half hour seem like a pathetic attempt to disguise my ulterior motive."

"Ask what?"

"Which I swear it's really not."

"Ask what?"

Zander squeezed my hand and looked up. "Quigley, do you think I could maybe kiss you?"

I couldn't really breathe, so I just nodded. Zander's hand smoothed the wisps of hair over my ear and gently pulled my face toward his. Our lips touched so softly I almost couldn't tell we were kissing until he leaned in against me. I felt his mouth curve into a smile against my cheek, which he also kissed, and then rested his forehead against mine for a second. "Thanks," he whispered.

I still wasn't doing so great with the breathing and talking thing, so I just nodded again.

He stared at me for a minute in the dark. I could see his smile as he turned the ignition. "We'd better get you home before Ms. Parisi calls to check how you're feeling and your parents freak out."

Chapter Ten

Click. Click. Click.

"Quigley?" Mrs. Albertt raised one eyebrow and looked pointedly at my shifting stool.

"Oops, sorry," I said.

"You're on duty supervising the developing lab after school. You might want to work on your focus," she said.

"Yes, ma'am."

I'd been staring at the same spot on the floor in front of me for most of class, avoiding David's attempts to catch my eye. When Anne and T-Shirt sat down at lunch, their company made it easy to scam my way out of dealing with the David talk, but in three short hours we'd be alone in the lab.

"I thought I showed all of the slides, but it appears there is one more," said Mrs. Albertt.

The titters from the class made me jump. I glanced at the

wall and then almost fell off my stool. The 5x8-foot image of David's smiling face above what looked like a dozen roses would have been shock enough had the foot-high letters PROM, QUIGLEY? not adorned the bottom of the shot.

A sinking feeling hit me as I turned to see David, standing at his table and pulling the identical roses out of his backpack.

"Well?" he asked with a cocky grin that let everyone in the room know he already knew my response would be yes. Before I could open my mouth, the class burst into applause and laughter. David took a little bow with a hand flourish. One of the guys got up to slap David on the back in congratulations. Even Mrs. Albertt smiled and offered David a little golf clap for his cleverness.

I felt a sudden rush of sisterhood with every woman in the world who has ever cluelessly attended a major sporting event, only to be surprised during halftime or the seventh-inning stretch by an unwelcome and very public scoreboard proposal. And like so many of my sisters, I caved to the peer pressure of what seemed like a thousand expectant faces and plastered on a fake smile while tightroping around how to pass without destroying the asker and ruining the enthusiasm of everyone involved.

If anyone had the strength to outright refuse the offer while surrounded by so many witnesses, well, it wasn't me. Instead of verbally accepting, which would have been too much like lying, I walked over and gave David a little half hug and took the flowers, setting off a chorus of "Woooooooo"'s until Mrs. Albertt admonished the class to bring our attention back to photography.

How had I spaced this? It had long been a tradition for seniors to compete in outdoing the rest of the class by coming up with crazy schemes to ask their crushes to prom. Just that morning, the letters on the backlit school sign at the parking lot entrance had been rearranged by a hopeful prom-goer asking her boyfriend to the dance. I never expected something like this from David so soon.

I kicked myself for not calling Anne and filling her in on the Zander developments immediately; she could have stopped this mess for me. I'd been so swept into the romance and thrill of Zander's kiss and declared interest, I wanted to protect the feeling and savor it untarnished before risking my best friend "Anne-alyzing" it. Big mistake. As it was, she'd probably encouraged David through T-Shirt, thinking she was doing me a favor.

I practically flew out the door when the bell rang.

"Quigley, wait up," David said.

"English exam," I called over my shoulder and kept moving.

It was a good thing David didn't know me better, or he'd never have bought my eagerness to get to class. As it turned out, neither did Mrs. Desmond.

"Quigley? What a surprise, you're early. This is good, I needed to have a word with you in private."

I walked in the classroom and slumped into a desk in front of her podium, stuffing the roses under my seat.

"Look, you're a good kid. You come on time and never miss an assignment. But you've got to start pulling your academic weight in this class. If you don't do well on the final, you'll be dangerously close to failing the course. I don't know what school you have in your sights, but it is not unheard of for universities to uninvite already accepted students."

"Yes, Mrs. Desmond." I decided not to point out that being uninvited wasn't a worry in my case. I wasn't exactly the queen of prefixes, but I knew enough to see it was hard to get *un*invited when you were never invited in the first place.

"I normally don't do this, but I want to give you a break. Would you be interested in some extra-credit work?"

I stifled a groan. "Sure, thank you."

"Don't look so worried. This is actually more creative than the technical work we've been doing lately. I've heard you have quite the talent for art, so maybe this will appeal to your right-brain mind-set."

She handed me a little booklet.

"Every year, the local Rotary Club invites each school in the state to submit one motivational speech from a student." She pointed at the teetering stacks of jumbled paperwork covering her desk. "I happen to be organizationally challenged, which is why this one slipped past me."

I smiled. It was refreshing to have a teacher admit a weakness.

"Unfortunately, the deadline is Friday. I know it doesn't give you much time, but I really won't be able to hold a contest to find this year's applicant in so short a period. If you're interested, I will just submit yours. What do you say? Knock this one out of the park, and it might significantly raise your grade and keep you from failing."

I wasn't much of a speechwriter, but with my records I could hardly turn down the offer. "Okay, sure. Thanks."

"By the way, nice flowers. This must be the magic day of madness. I had a costumed Puck singing telegram show up in my fourth-period AP lit class. Put to shame yesterday's student jumping onto his desk to perform the opening of the *Romeo and Juliet* balcony scene—so trite. Ah, iambic-pentameter prom invites—what will you kids come up with next?"

• • • • • • • • • • • •

The rest of the day went by in a blur. I had several conversations with imaginary David in my mind during current affairs and trig, while ducking corners and jogging up deserted back staircases to avoid the real one. The dialogue went pretty well, but I wasn't so sure how the discussion would go *outside* of my head. Anne stopped by my locker for a brief end-of-the-day check-in. She wore a bright yellow, too small T-shirt with a giant YES!!!! across the chest.

"Do I even want to know?" I asked, pointing at her outfit.

"Present from T."

"Of course."

"Did I hear my name?" T-Shirt strolled down the hall, stopping just long enough to swing in and kiss Anne for about thirty seconds longer than was comfortable to stand watching.

"Ah," I said, pointing to the YO, ANNE——WE GOING TO PROM OR WHAT? across his back. "Nice."

T-Shirt came up for air with a smile. "Thanks! I heard David did the deed. Done deal. You girls pick out the grub spot; we've got transpo covered. I know a guy."

"I'm sure you do."

T-Shirt gave Anne an endearing good-bye swat on the butt and continued down the hall.

"Excellent!" Anne squealed. "This is so great! Isn't it great?"

I checked to make sure T-Shirt was out of earshot. "No. We need to talk."

The locker next to me erupted into a woman's sultry voice loudly singing a suggestive chorus of "Say Yes," startling the girl spinning in her combination, as well as everyone within ten feet, except for the guy holding a little MP3 remote, and the cluster of his buddies high-fiving his success half-way down the hall. She opened the door to the little player wrapped up with a big bow and her own friends' "Awww"s.

"I've got to get out of here." I pulled Anne into the bath-room for enough privacy to fill her in and debate my options on getting out of the mess.

"I'm just going to be honest with David," I said for the third time.

This made her roll her eyes, for the third time. "I'm telling you, guys don't want to hear they are getting ditched over some other guy."

"He's already seen me with Zander. It won't be a huge shock. I'll just tell him I wasn't expecting our day of shooting to be anything but two friends taking pictures in the park."

"So much for honesty. Didn't he pretty much ask you specifically on a date?"

"Oh, right." I'd forgotten my "I'm going on a date, on a date, on a date" litany from the other day. Not to mention his flower.

"Trust me. Make up something about how busy you are right now. Use that speech as an excuse. People understand heavy workloads when you're trying to get into a college. He'll back off, and this way you haven't hurt his feelings. There's time yet—I'll help you nail down Zander for the dance. Once David asks someone else, it won't be a big deal how things shake out. It's the only way to go. Just whatever you do, don't bring up the fact there's another guy. I know about these things."

"Yeah, well, last time you *knew about these things*, I talked myself into thinking Zander wasn't into me. Which is why I'm in this mess to begin with."

"You make a good point. But what do you have to lose? If you just brush David off in general, you don't have to worry about what Zander will think, because there will be nothing happening between you and David, right?".

"I guess. I gotta go, David'll be waiting."

Anne gave me a quick hug. "Good luck! Come by backstage after if you want and dish all the gory details."

"You're enjoying this all a little too much," I said.

"Yep!" She laughed and headed toward the theater.

I took the long way to the art room, less than eager to share the latest developments with David. Part of me hoped he'd be gone when I got there or think he had the time wrong. But he was sitting on the counter smiling and twirling the keys to the opened darkroom on one finger when I walked in. Despite Anne's advice, I still thought the best way to handle this situation was to be totally honest.

"Hey, you. I've hardly seen you today," he said. "Mrs. Albertt left the keys with me. She was very impressed I stayed to help you."

"Heh, I bet. It's been a crazy day."

I gathered up twelve rolls of film from the class, along with the three we had taken at the park. Even with David's help, I'd need to have four or five developing tubs going at once if we were going to finish by dinner.

"So, what do we do first? Turn on the warning light, right?" he asked.

He flipped the switch that turned on the red lightbulb placed above the door outside the room. No one would open the door and ruin the photographs while it was lit.

I almost groaned aloud. This also meant no one could leave the room. I spaced that. As I heard the door click behind us, I realized Anne's method of dealing with this mess might be best, considering that David and I were going to be stuck together in here for the next two hours.

"Give me the list. I need to check it. Earlier, I prepared the chemicals we would need—developer, stop bath, fixer—by mixing them as instructed. I also secured the negatives, so we can run two processes at once to save time." I handed him the instruction sheet to look over, and launched into the easy letdown. "So, I've been running like crazy today, but I wanted to talk to you."

"Yeah, I noticed that. No time for your boy at all. Guess you girls have a lot to sort out for the dance."

I glanced at the sheet and squinted. "Did we make sure that the temperature of the chemicals is at least sixty-eight degrees? Let's place the containers in a pan of several inches of water to regulate that. These negatives are just about ready to splice." I handed the tube to David. "Well, that's sort of the thing," I continued. "I really don't have time right now. Remember when we were talking about colleges? The thing is, I don't have many options to choose from."

"I'm sorry. Here I was going on and on about where I might go and who I turned down. No wonder you got all weird."

I ignored the comments and continued reading from the worksheet. "So we organized the equipment so that you can find them in the dark. Got the film reel, film container, and scissors for cutting the film from the film spool? Let's flash these others while we're doing that to save time . . . and make sure I'm not making a total mess of this."

I was making a total mess of this. He'd probably never understand my real feelings about his choice, but that didn't matter. He seemed to understand the college pressures, so I went with what was working. "Yeah. I'm just really stressed, but it looks like I might have a way out. It's going to take work and time. A *lot* of work and time. Like, too much energy to get wrapped up in something with you right now. I hope you understand.

"We're developing several rolls at once, so fill the developing tank with developer almost to the top. These should be transferring now—here we go, and here they are!" I pointed down at the images, slowly coming into focus on the wet paper.

"So you're a girl with focus. I get it. It's all good, Quigley." He ribbed me with a wink and an exaggerated Art King smirk. "After all, I can see how a girl could get too distracted by my charms."

I smiled. "Thanks for understanding, David."

So Anne was right. I had stopped things with David without hurting his feelings. Now I could see what might happen with Zander without guilt hanging over my head. Perfect. By the time prom rolled around, David would have moved on to Maria or whoever he ended up asking.

"Wow, awesome. That one came out exactly like what we were going for!" David said.

"You're right. But something's missing. The ones in the museum seemed like everything was stopping for a reason. These just look like blurred action shots."

"True," he said. "But we're definitely close."

"I think so. Now we just hang them to dry."

I tensed as David's body came up behind me in the dark. He smelled like peanut butter and Dr Pepper. I felt his breath on my neck about a second before he started kissing it. I yelped and dropped the photo. I jumped backward into David as the liquid in the tub splashed on me.

"Crap! What's in these chemicals?" I patted down the table looking for a towel to wipe off my wet arms and shirt.

"How should I know? You're supposed to be the expert here, Teach'. Why'd you jump like that, anyway?" David slid his arms back around my waist. "It's all good. We've got the place to ourselves."

I peeled his arms off me and turned around to face him. "I thought we just talked about this."

"Sure. You're busy and tied up with school stuff, priorities, yadda-yadda. But this is perfect. Here we are, *in* school, doing school stuff—it's like the ultimate in multitasking!"

He leaned in for a kiss.

"There's this other guy," I blurted.

David stopped cold. "Other guy?"

"Well, yes. It's not anything to do with you—"

"You're stopping me from kissing you right now. So it seems like it does have a little something to do with me."

"No, I mean. I was hanging out with him first, and then things got—"

"Wait. Is this the guy I saw you with at the exhibit?" David took a step back. "You know, the exhibit *I* invited you to?"

"Umm."

"Gotcha."

"You don't understand."

He gave a bitter laugh. "Oh, I think I do. I'm outta here."

He slammed the door open. The flash of bright outside light made me wince. I spun around to see all the carefully half-developed images floating in the tubs slowly disappear. My hopes of untangling the mess without hurting anyone vanished as quickly as the hard work of my classmates.

· · · · · · · · · · · ·

I barely had the strength to dial Anne's number. Jogging home after spending almost four hours in a lab swirling and hanging and squeegeeing a million photos, for the second time, was a stupid idea. It had been so long since I rode the bus I forgot the schedule. I really needed a car.

Anne picked up on the second ring.

"So where were you earlier? I waited at the theater the whole afternoon," Anne said.

"Let's just say things didn't go so great with David."

"You went and told him about Zander, didn't you?"

I peeled off my sock and inspected my heel for blisters. "Well—"

"Quigley! I told you."

"Okay, fine. This time you were right."

"So it was bad."

"Well, I wouldn't be making plans for that joint limo to prom."

I could hear the British accents of some BBC sitcom coming from her TV, followed by clicking as she channel surfed.

"When are you going to ask Zander?"

"I'm not sure. Is he too old? I mean, will he think it's completely stupid?"

"He's only eighteen."

"Is he? He seems so much more mature. How did you know that and I didn't?"

"I snuck a look through Mom's records to check out The Spikester's details. How'd you think I found out about the kid? Anyway, he's having a birthday in two weeks!"

"The Spikester? What's he going to be, thirty-four?"

"Hardy har har. No. *Your* man. I was checking his sign— you two are totally compatible, by the way. A week from next

Thursday he'll turn nineteen. But that's only a couple years older than you are, no biggie. It's not like he doesn't know we're still in high school."

"I guess so. Man, I can't believe it's his birthday. What am I going to get him?"

"Don't worry, I'll help you find something perfect. We need to go try on some dresses anyway. We can do it this weekend. Oh, before I forget—The Spikester set us up with a sweet side gig."

"Babysitting?"

She snorted. "So, so funny. He's got this RISD grad bud who branched off and started creating these crazy, fantastical performance art programs."

"Anne, my days as a dead body are over."

"No, nothing like that. Well, okay—they do improv and scripted scenes sometimes, but they also do parade work. There's a big Earth Day parade downtown and they've signed on for it, but his troupe could use some extras. It's supposed to be very *Midsummer's Night Dream* on acid."

"Lovely."

"It will be! The sprites even get harnessed up to flit around high up on the float. The Spikester is helping with the costumes, and he says he thought of me the whole time he did this one shimmery-fairy bodysuit."

"TMI, Anne. TMI."

"Wait, you won't believe this. The Spikester told the guy about me and the guy said I was in, so then—and now you can feel guilty—he tells the guy I have this really cool best friend and is there a place for you? And the guy says, 'Can she play a piccolo?'"

"*No!*"

"Yes!"

I thought back to when Anne and I first met, in line for instrument signup for third-grade band. A short, freckled kid lumbered past us, weighed down by a massive tuba. Anne leaned over and whispered, "Piccolo." "Piccolo?" I whispered back. She glanced around to make sure no one else could benefit from her genius. "Think of the walk to the bus." She held out a pinky. I hesitated just a moment before extending mine with a nod and starting what would be a lifelong tradition of blindly following Anne's questionable advice.

"So I tell him—Quigley? Quigley can *rock* a piccolo! She'll play the best piccolo in the history of the parade."

"Anne, piccolo was *hard*! It was the worst. Four months

and we never even once hit a decent note. They made us switch to the cowbell."

"Maybe they just needed more cowbell. What does it matter anyway? You'll get the forty bucks and fake it. The rest of the instruments will drown you out."

I pulled the laces loose on my other running shoe. "Anne, can I ask you something without you getting pissed?"

"When you start out like that, probably not," she laughed.

"I'm just wondering. Do you think we're being a little silly about the dress thing?"

There was a moment of silence on the line. "What do you mean?"

"Well, it's just a lot of money to waste on something your mom would be happy to make us for free."

"That's not the point. It's the principle of the thing, Quigley! I thought you were with me on this. Where's the best-friend support?"

"I know. It was just that Zander told me the other night how he bought his car for only four hundred dol—"

"Gawd, Quigley. You're not going to be that kind of girl who is always spouting 'my boyfriend said this' and 'my boyfriend did that' now, are you?"

I blushed at the *B*-word. "No! I just thought it seemed like something real to hold on to, compared to a dress we can really only wear the one time."

"Fine. You go find yourself a car for four hundred bucks. I'm sticking with the plan. If I'm feeling generous, I'll pull over in the limo and give you a ride when I see you broken down on the side of the road. But no promises."

I sighed. "You're pissed."

"Of course, I'm pissed. We've been working at this for months now. You wouldn't have even *met* your guy if it weren't for my Betterment Plan and getting us this gig with my mom. Now you're backing out."

"No, I'm not. I swear. I was just bringing it up for discussion," I said.

"Well, are we done discussing?"

"Totally."

"Look, I know you think my mom is the best thing in the world, and so cool and everything, but it's a lot different from where I'm sit—*oh no*."

"Anne?"

The only thing I could hear through the phone was the sound of her tabloid news program.

"Anne? Hello?" The faint laughter sounded different from

her usual deep belly laugh. "Anne? What's so funny?"

It took a minute to recognize the sound as sobs. In nine years of knowing her, I had never heard my best friend cry like that. My chest ached with panic. "Anne, talk to me. Hello? What's going on?" The tabloid show droned on in the background. I pressed the phone so hard against my ear that it went numb and caught the newscaster in the background mention the name Gordon.

"I'm right here, Anne. Tell me what's going on. No matter what, everything's going to be okay. *Okay?*" I tried to steady my voice as I frantically flipped through the channels to see what her dear old dad was up to now.

The phone slid from my hand as his smiling voice came across the screen. "Sexiest man alive turned sexiest dad alive, Keith Gordon has confirmed he and his adopted child will be returning to the United States as soon as the paperwork is completed. Keith Gordon is quoted as saying he's always wanted to be a father, and would appreciate being given privacy and the opportunity to bond with his new daughter outside of the public arena."

"I'll be right there, Anne."

• • • • • • • • • • • • • • • • • • • •

Chapter Eleven

I peeled several bills off and stuffed them in the cab-driver's hand. Having no clue if you were supposed to tip or not, I put an extra two wrinkled ones on top of the fare and ran up Anne's drive and hit the doorbell. I fidgeted and stabbed at the bell two more times and peered into the foyer, which appeared broken into prismatic shards through the ornamental glass door. Ms. Parisi's car wasn't in the driveway, so I let myself in.

"Anne?"

I raced up the stairs toward the muffled sobs. Something heavy leaned against Anne's door, but I managed to nudge it enough to stick my head in. Her nightstand was knocked over, and shredded confetti covered her lime-green rug and black bedspread. I took in what must have been hundreds of ripped-up magazine pages. Pushing my way in, I lifted a piece and recognized the trademark smile and chin dimple Anne didn't inherit from her mom. The mounted flat screen had a deep dent that matched the broken vase lying lopsided on the dresser beneath it.

"I'm so sorry, Anne."

"How could he?" The small voice came from the floor of the closet. I waded through the piles of paper and tried to hug the huddled lump that was my friend. She flinched at my touch and hugged her knees to her chest tighter.

"I don't know. I'm so sorry." Why hadn't I called Ms. Parisi? What could I say to make this better?

"How could he?" she demanded. "I want to know! How could he throw me away? It should have been me!" Her fists pounded the closet walls, and she spun around and kicked the neatly stacked shoe boxes into crumpled cardboard pieces. *"Why didn't he want me?"* Her clunky military-style boots stomped the boxes against the wall with each word before she dove back into a ball of hysterical sobs.

I swiped at the hot tears now running down my face. "I don't know." I reached out and touched her trembling leg. "I'm so sorry." I winced at the stupid useless phrase.

I hadn't realized I'd been holding my breath until the startling hollow bang of the front door followed by the mad click of heels up the stairs made me suck in air.

"Anne! Anne, honey! Honey, I have to tell you some—" Ms. Parisi's faking-calm face peeked around the door. She'd wiped away her bleeding mascara, but telltale pale streaks ran down her cheeks where her own tears had washed away her makeup. "Oh God. You heard. Honey? Baby. Baby, it's going to be okay."

"Okay?" Anne struggled through the broken boxes and lunged out of the closet. "Okay?"

I slid back against Anne's DANGEROUS CURVES sign, wishing I could disappear.

"Nothing is okay! You ruined it. You ruined everything!" Anne's face was a blotchy purply red. "If you meant anything to him at all, he would have wanted to be my dad. I always knew he wanted me; he just couldn't stand to be around you. This is your fault! I hate you! I hate you!"

Anne's heavy boots clomped down the stairs. Ms. Parisi jerked at the slam of the door and slid to the paper-littered bed in defeat. She picked up a handful of the torn pages as a bitter laugh turned to a sob.

I stayed frozen against the wall. Grown-ups weren't supposed to cry in front of kids.

"She'll be back in a few minutes," I finally said in a low voice.

She nodded and wiped her wet cheek and took a deep breath.

"I didn't even know she collected these." Ms. Parisi tried to put the pieces together and then swept away the jagged, smiling face with a sigh.

"It wasn't like that, you know," she said, picking up and stroking a particularly large slashed piece featuring the famous man's left eye and cheek with an expression near regret. "We were just kids. It wasn't about wanting, or not wanting. What eighteen-year-old kid wants to be a dad? We both thought we were going places. We *knew* it. I mean, everyone knew they were going places back in those days, but, luck of the draw, for both of us it turned out to be true. Marrying a stranger and playacting some happy-family routine wasn't going to get us to where we belonged. We both agreed. It wasn't the time. So we went our separate ways." She let the image flutter to the floor, her eyes pleading for understanding. "I just . . . changed my mind."

I patted her back and felt our roles shift. After a minute

of awkward silence, I pulled over Anne's black leather trash can and lifted handfuls of the torn paper into it. Ms. Parisi joined me, and we cleaned the room together, silently lost in our own thoughts.

We relocated to the living room and sipped ineffectual herbal tea whose box promised it to be "calming." Ms. Parisi started at every sound outside, but the afternoon light faded and Anne still hadn't reappeared. "Quigley, would you mind trying again?"

"No problem, Ms. Parisi." I hit redial to call Anne's cell.

"Victoria," she corrected absently, and continued staring at the window with glazed eyes.

"No answer."

"Is it still turned off?" she asked.

"It went right to voice mail."

"Do you think you could stay? I'll call your parents and let them know, if you want me to," she said, her shaky voice lacking its usual command.

I nodded. "You don't need to tell them about, well—you know. I can just say you were making dinner or something. Or that Anne and I wanted to study."

We looked at each other. It struck us at the same time how unlikely either of the two excuses sounded, and we burst into laughter. We laughed harder and harder until tears flowed from the release of the afternoon's tension. The reflection of blue-and-red lights spiraling across the darkened wall interrupted our giggles.

"Oh God, no!" Ms. Parisi had run in a panic through the door in her stocking feet before I even recognized the flashing lights as those of a police car.

Chapter Twelve

• • • • • • • • • • • • • • • • •

"Are you the mother of Anastasia Gordon Parisi?" asked the officer.

Anne's mother rocked on her feet and looked like she might pass out. "She is," I yelped and grabbed her shoulders as the officer dove to support Ms. Parisi's crumpling body.

"Ms. Parisi! Ms. Parisi, your daughter is fine," he said. "We came down as a courtesy due to your public persona and the possibility of media interference once this story breaks fully."

"She's okay?" Ms. Parisi's voice squeaked out, desperate for reassurance as she gripped the man's uniform. "My Anne's okay?"

He nodded, and together we helped her lean against the patrol car to regain her composure.

"Ma'am, you need to call an attorney for your daughter. She's been arrested on multiple charges, some of which could prove quite serious. Unfortunately, some of the evidence has already gone public; a video was posted to the Internet. Kids." He shook his head. "When we realized she was the daughter of such a noted public figure—"

"She told you?" Ms. Parisi and I gasped simultaneously.

The officer looked at us with a puzzled expression. "Yes, ma'am. You are her mother, are you not?" He flipped open a little notebook. "Victoria Parisi? We helped you out a few months ago with those photographers?"

"Oh, me. Yes, I'm a public figure. I mean, yes. Yes, I'm her mother. I see."

I hoped the officer assumed her incoherence came from shock. My heart thudded at how close we had both come to letting slip the secret that could forever change life in the Parisi home.

"Ma'am. Pardon me for saying this, but you don't seem to be in any shape to drive." He looked around as concerned neighbors—unused to the sight of a police car in their conservative, well-to-do enclave—peered through windows and open front doors. "We seem to already be attracting a fair amount of attention. Perhaps you'd like to hop in and we can bring you down to the station? You can contact your attorney from there, if you like."

Ms. Parisi nodded and turned to me. "Can you? Would you mind?"

"Of course," I said, and took her trembling hand.

The officer turned off the flashing lights and opened the back door. I slid in onto a hard plastic molded seat. The rough nonskid material gave me a bit of rug burn as I scooted across to make room for Ms. Parisi.

She climbed in, still dazed, feeling the spot where a door handle would have been and took in her unlikely surroundings. "There are no seat belts."

"No, ma'am. Injury risk."

I tried to block out the images of those who had previously occupied this seat as the officer pulled away from the house and headed toward the main road. He picked up the radio to report the presence of two passengers en route to the station.

I took advantage of his distraction to whisper to Ms. Parisi. "*Gordon?* I thought her middle name was Guinevere. Why would you risk—"

She leaned close. "At the time, I thought it would be a nice memento." She waved away the absurdity of her words. "I'm sure the morphine from the C-section didn't help my reasoning powers at the time. I romantically thought she'd appreciate the nod to her parentage down the road. How was I supposed to know that before she was even old enough to realize she had a middle name, *his* would be plastered all around the world? Obviously, there was *a lot* about that time in my life I hadn't thought through."

"But Anne hates 'Guinevere'—you always said her middle name was a family name."

"In a way, it was." Ms. Parisi shrugged off the irony with a weary sigh. "What was I going to do? I don't lie to my daughter, Quigley, but this is one little detail she's not fully aware of."

"I don't understand."

"Just one of those things that wasn't an issue, until suddenly it was. He hit it big about the same time I had to register her for kindergarten. It seemed so insignificant; I just changed it on the paperwork to 'Guinevere.' She was already a bit of a spark plug, and I hoped she'd never be tempted to use such an old-fashioned name. The Department of Motor Vehicles only uses a middle initial, so it just never really came up."

"Until now."

"Until now." She nodded. "I don't know what's going on here, but let's just hope it's not anything that draws too much attention. My God, do you have any idea what she might be up to?"

My mind went straight to T-Shirt's crew, but I didn't want to rat my best friend out if it was something completely different. Considering Anne's mood, it could be anything. Still, my loyalty to Ms. Parisi pulled at me.

"Here we are," the officer said, saving me from the tough call.

· · · · · · · · · · · ·

The officer ushered us through a back door into a long hallway that smelled faintly of ammonia. The blank, cream-painted concrete walls and antiseptic square offices reminded me more of a hospital or school than what I would have imagined a police station to be like . He stopped in front of a room with a single, large glass window facing the hall. Tiny lines of steel ran through the glass creating a diamond pattern you'd notice only if you were actively trying to ignore the view through the pane. A pale and defeated Anne sat hunched over on a bench in the otherwise empty room. She looked half her age.

"She's right in here. We haven't processed her yet. We wanted to reach you before the media did. It's not procedure, but if you'd like to have a few words? Then you can call your attorney, and we have some paperwork you need to fill out." He turned to me. "I'm sorry, but you'll need to stay here."

I nodded, strangely relieved. Down the hall, a tall man wearing a suit even I could tell was expensive had his arm protectively around T-Shirt's shoulders as they walked to what appeared to be the main desk. Two other suits carrying man bags blatantly ignored the NO CELL PHONES signs and flanked the pair. The grim-faced officer seemed unimpressed by T-Shirt's entourage, perhaps due to the day's words of cottony wisdom: WHERE ARE WE GOING? AND WHY AM I IN THIS HANDBASKET?

Inside, Ms. Parisi plastered Anne's face with kisses and smothered her to her chest.

A matronly, uniformed woman approached. "I'm ready for her now."

The officer cracked the door. "Ms. Parisi, we'll need you to come handle some paperwork." He turned to Anne. "Officer Munroe will take you to get your fingerprints and photographs for the file."

Ms. Parisi flinched at *fingerprints*. She clung to Anne's arm for a moment before giving her a quick hug and kissing her forehead with a pained fake smile of reassurance. Officer

Munroe's far more believable kind and businesslike smile helped ease the tension as she led Anne past us to another room. I touched Anne's arm lightly, but my presence didn't even register on her exhausted face.

I sat in the cold office chair and wrapped my legs around the metal legs to stretch. Ms. Parisi spoke heatedly into her cell phone, earning a nasty look from the desk. As she stepped outside to finish her call, the realization hit that I had somehow ended an otherwise lousy day sitting all by myself in a strange police station.

"Shouldn't be long now," Ms. Parisi said. Her perfect lip liner smudged as she absently bit her lip. "I can't tell you what it means to have you here."

I reached out and squeezed her clenched hands, triggering her ragged intake of breath I feared might turn into a sob. She composed herself and stared straight ahead, still clutching my hand hard enough to leave faint crescent marks from her manicured nails.

After what seemed to be hours, Ms. Parisi's attorney secured the necessary permissions from a judge, and we prepared to leave the station and the ordeal behind us, for the moment.

"Thankfully, Anne's still a minor. Public access to the

police reports should be restricted, as long as there aren't any leaks," Ms. Parisi said as we waited for Anne's official release. She lowered her voice. "Including her full name and mug—well, images."

I nodded and yawned.

"Poor thing, I'm sorry for keeping you so long. Thank you for being here with me, you're a good friend—to us both," she said. "I've called a cab. I think the neighborhood's had enough excitement for one day without any more patrol car appearances. It's probably not the best night to stay over. Can we drop you on our way?"

"Actually, I'm way out of your way. Anne probably just wants to get home. I think I'll try Zander, if it's okay."

Ms. Parisi smiled. "Just check in with your parents first, okay, Quigley? We like to know where you girls are."

"Okay, Ms. Parisi."

Zander's phone rang nine times. It was really late. Maybe he was sleeping. But it clicked the way it does when someone hits ignore—strange, since Zander always clicked over to tell me if he was tied up. I hung up, checked the number, and tried again.

"Hi, Quigley—what's up."

His tone certainly didn't sound sleepy. It wasn't exactly

annoyed, but there was an unfamiliar clipped note that left the impression he wasn't thrilled with the call. My cheeks flamed. What was I thinking calling him so late out of the blue?

"I'm sorry to call so late—"

"It's fine. What did you need?"

I stammered as his all-business attitude made my mind go blank.

"Um, nothing. It's fine. It was just— Look, it's nothing. Never mind, sorry I called."

There was an awkward silence. He took a deep breath and let it out slowly. When he spoke, the usual warm, caring Zander returned.

"Quigley, it's after midnight. You're not a phone person and have only ever called to make arrangements for something. Are you okay?"

"Yes. I mean, well, not really. But it's fine. You're busy or something. No worries. I'm just at this police station—"

"*What?* Which one?"

"I don't know the name, the one down near the convention center."

"I'll be right there."

I joined Ms. Parisi by the back door as they led Anne

down the hall. She rushed forward on seeing her mom and dove into her arms, crying into her shoulder. I took a step back, feeling out of place in the midst of such a personal family moment, but Ms. Parisi's hand reached out and pulled me back into a group hug.

"You okay?" I asked Anne.

She nodded, looking shell-shocked.

"Let's get you home," Ms. Parisi said. "Quigley, did you need a ride?"

"Zander's on his way. He lives right off campus—should be here any minute."

"We'll wait until he arrives. Maybe we'd all like some fresh air?" Ms. Parisi pushed open the door and then jerked back at the series of flashes from outside. She instinctively lurched in front of Anne as a few photographers called out her name, eager to get their shot.

An officer pushed past us to clear away the cameras. "Sorry, ma'am—it's a restricted area. Should have been empty."

"Great. I don't even have makeup on," Anne attempted to joke with a wan smile.

Through the door we heard the officer's voice threaten

trespassing charges for anyone remaining in the authorized-access only area. A moment later, he stepped back in.

"Used to see a fair amount of this when I worked in New York. Not often we have to deal with this sort of thing around here," he said. "They should all be cleared out. Looks like your cab is waiting."

Officer Munroe approached from the front of the station. "I have an Alexander Macintosh at the desk for Ms. Quigley Johnson."

"Are you going to be okay?" Ms. Parisi asked me.

"I'm fine. Are you going to be at school tomorrow, Anne?" I asked.

She looked to her mom, who answered for her. "It's late. I think we may take a personal day. I'll cancel my appointments. Maybe we'll order in Chinese and watch some reality shows or something?"

Anne nodded with a small smile.

"You're welcome to join us after school, Quigley."

"Thanks, that sounds nice." I couldn't help grinning at the thought of Ms. Parisi watching reality TV. Her taste ran more to PBS literary specials and the History Channel.

The sight of Zander's frumpled plaid pajama pants and

baggy long-sleeve tee caught me off guard. I had never seen him as anything but meticulously put together. His worried eyes crinkled as they followed my gaze down to his . . . flip-flops?

He shrugged, chagrined. "I just jumped in the car."

"Apparently." I couldn't help smiling. He was adorable. I couldn't resist and went in for a hug. "Thank you," I said into his chest.

Leaning up against the thin material of his tee revealed the unexpected tautness of a closet athlete. My hand slid over his shoulder to pull him closer and rubbed on a thick knobby seam of what must have been a tank underneath. He shifted my hand to rest against his neck. The familiar scent of his barely there cologne soothed my nerves, and I was suddenly exhausted.

"Umm, Quigley? This is a nice, romantic moment and all, but maybe this isn't the best place?"

I pulled back and caught sight of a sprinkling of strangers, there for who knows what reason, eyeing us.

"You're probably right."

"I brought my ID and my checkbook. Who do we need to talk to? And where are your parents?"

"What? Oh no. It's not me. My parents think I'm staying

over at Anne's—it's a long story. Let's get out of here and I'll tell you on the way home."

I waved good-bye to Officer Munroe and pulled a confused Zander out into the street. Two guys with cameras hung around their necks chatted while leaning against an old Volvo. I hoped their loitering meant that they hadn't gotten their shot and that Anne and Ms. Parisi had made it home unbothered. Zander studied me as he unlocked and opened my door. I slid in and reached across the seats to unlock his side as he walked around the tiny car.

He smiled as he settled in. "Just passed my first test."

"First test?"

"Well, shouldn't say first. But a significant one."

"You're testing me now?"

"*Test* is a strong word. There are just a few little things that people do that tell you a lot about their character. So if one was, say, trying to determine if a girl he admires would click in his life in a slightly more serious way, the tiniest act, or lack thereof, might reveal more about who she really is. Better than playing Twenty Questions every time you go out on a date. Besides, I'm naïve. People fool me because I tend to only see the best in them."

I grinned, having no idea about what he was talking about, but tickled by the "click in his life" talk. The comment gave me just enough confidence to ask him to prom . . . when the right moment came up.

"And I passed?"

"Flying colors." He smiled and pulled away from the station up to a red light. "Don't worry, it's not like I'd have ditched you as a friend or judged you if you hadn't. But a little thing like unlocking my door, instead of making me use my key shows that even when your mind must be at its most frazzled, you still managed to think about someone else. Impressive. Of course, I *did* just pick you up in the middle of the night from a police station . . . demonstration the system isn't foolproof."

He reached over and slid the backs of his fingers down my cheek, before pulling my chin toward his and kissing me lightly, square on the mouth. How did he do that so smoothly that I didn't even have time for nerves to kick in? Postsmooch butterflies hit, and I tried to regain my composure as we moved through the now-green light into the empty streets of the city.

"Seriously though, Quigley, what on earth was that all about?"

I didn't anticipate how tough it might be to stay loyal to Anne while explaining the middle-of-the-night ride request. Spilling the goods about her dad was out of the question. But without understanding the devastation caused by his adoption news, whatever crazy mess Anne had gotten herself into would just sound all the more insane. I didn't want my maybe-boyfriend to start out our relationship thinking terrible things about my best friend. And really, with the day she'd had, she deserved to have somebody protecting her.

"Kind of a long story. I'm not clear on all the details. Just a bit of a scrape Anne fell into, no biggie." Maybe a change of subject would work. "So, when I called the first time, you didn't pick up. I hope I didn't wake you."

His mouth tightened, and there was a little twitch at one corner of his lips.

"I had a rough day. I was on the other line with someone hashing it out," he said, and promptly went back. "A scrape? Hmm. 'No biggie' doesn't usually land you or your best friend in trouble with the cops."

I ignored the comment. "Pretty late, lucky your someone was still around to help." Though his vagueness in the mention of the mysterious "someone" made me curious, I was more in deflect mode than dig mode.

"They're on West Coast time. Long day, long story—I don't really want to go into it all, okay?" He smiled apologetically and took my hand to soften the brush-off. "What I would love to know is what exactly qualifies as a no-big-deal scrape in your book."

I sighed. The truth was I didn't even know what she'd done. I suspected her earlier rage led her to jump in on the ultimate collecting expedition, stealing the light bar from the top of the mean cop's car. On the off chance Zander subscribed to the theory "Birds of a feather, flock together," I wasn't ready to admit my closest friend was that nuts. The officer's comments about serious charges fit, though, since stealing from the actual police probably qualifies as a little bigger deed than simple sign vandalism.

"Vandalism," I said, downplaying it. "I mean, I assume it was. Ms. Parisi left me in the waiting room when they were discussing the details with the police, so I don't have the whole story yet. But T-Shirt—the guy she's been hanging out with lately—and his friends do that kind of thing."

"What guy? I thought she was with Lance."

"Who's Lance?"

"Lance! Lance, from class." He laughed at my blank look.

"Lance, who she's been seeing since class began?"

"The Spikester's name is *Lance*?" Maybe it was my exhaustion, but this struck me as hysterically funny.

"You're laughing at my friend for being named Lance at the same time you're telling me your friend's cheating on him with some guy named after an article of clothing?"

This made me laugh even harder. Zander just shook his head in mock dismay and absently rubbed our intertwined knuckles under his chin with a chuckle. The slight scratch of his stubble gave me goose bumps, and I wished away the sight of my street sign just ahead.

"In all seriousness, I hope you're reading the situation wrong with Anne. Lance is a good guy. He's had a lot of crap dealt to him in life, and he really likes her. That class and connecting with Anne has been a rare escape for him. She's not into him? Fine, but be straight with the guy. He deserves his one night out a week not to end up crushing him."

"C'mon. One night a week? A guy like that is probably out every night until the wee hours."

"He is." Zander put the car in park and kissed my hand. He turned to me and leaned back against the driver's-side window. "Working. He pulls the night shift, nine to three a.m., seven nights a week down at the Body Shop."

"The tattoo and piercing place? Must be like a total party in there."

"Maybe. Does that make it any less admirable? I know he loves his work. He designs original body art, like when people come in and describe what they want without a picture. He creates the piece for the actual tattoo artists to use."

"Explains his image."

"Maybe that's just Lance. But even so, the guy underneath is about as good as it gets as far as I'm concerned. He does it all for his son."

Seven days a week was pretty intense. "Yeah, Anne said he had a kid when he was super young."

"I just think it's amazing he gets by on five hours of sleep while chasing after a four-year-old all day. He never says it, but I think some part of him has to be stoked that kindergarten's coming up next year. I think that's why he made the push to finish his degree this semester. He'll be able to take a job with more regular hours, maybe even move out of his folks' basement."

"He is hardly the type I'd expect to still be living with his parents." I cringed at my tone. I didn't know much about Zander's living situation.

"What can you do? Your high school sweetheart takes off and leaves you with a newborn, you have to make a few adjustments to the ol' life plan. What a transition, though. I don't know how he did it and kept such a good attitude. He had his own place, but moved back home so his parents could help watch the baby after they got home from work and he could make some cash knowing the baby was safe."

"My God, he has sole custody?" I gave myself a little mental kick for every ungenerous thought or comment I'd made in The Spikester's direction.

"Yep. She relinquished her parental rights and left town straight from the hospital and never looked back. Wanted no part of that life. Most guys would have dumped the kid on their parents and kept up the partying life. He doesn't even use day care."

"I cannot imagine taking on that kind of responsibility—dealing with your whole life imploding when you're that young!"

"Well, sometimes you expect Lemon Yellow and life gives you Burnt Sienna. You still have to make the best picture you can with what you've got," said Zander.

We sat in silence and watched the neighbor's streetlamp flicker. I hoped the sudden sadness in Zander's eyes would fade away, and he'd kiss me again. Then I could ask him about the dance. I looked up at the darkened windows of my house and felt a twinge of guilt, knowing my parents thought I was safely tucked in bed at Anne's.

"Or maybe just let your four-year-old eat the offending 'crayon of life'?"

He snorted and shook off whatever dark thoughts had floated into his head. Without thinking I leaned in for a peck of my own, earning a full return of his smile.

"So, look. If Anne is all stuck on spray-paint-toting Tank Top, maybe she can let Lance down easy? Or better yet, reconsider what a great guy she'll be missing out on over some juvenile delinquent with a taste for tagging."

"Oh, he's not into graffiti. They just go on collecting expeditions."

He leaned toward me and tugged on one lock of hair with a smile. His breath was warm in my ear.

"Mmm. Even better—stealing from unlocked cars in parking lots? What a winner." The sarcasm shone through his whisper.

His lips grazing my neck made it difficult to speak. This was pretty new territory for me. Maybe I shouldn't be trying.

"No, nothing like that. They just swipe street signs."

The almost-kisses suddenly stopped.

"What?"

Not sure how to fix the broken mood, I tried to stay light. "Not a big deal, just a few street signs. Anne's got one up in her bedroom." Zander pulled back. I got a sudden chill from more than the absence of his lips on my skin.

Zander slid back upright, facing the wheel. It's tough to gauge someone's expression from his profile in the dark.

"How did you know about her sign?" His words came slowly.

"I saw it a few weeks ago." I reached out and squeezed his hand. He didn't pull away, but it stayed limply balanced on the gear shift. "What's wrong?"

"What, like 'Main Street,' 'Anne Street,' something like that?"

"Umm, not really that kind. This one said, DANGEROUS CURVES."

I flinched at his sharp intake of breath.

"What did Ms. Parisi say about the sign?"

"Well, nothing. I don't think Anne lets her mom into her room."

"And you didn't tell her?" Zander's voice trembled.

"No," I stammered. "She's my friend. You don't go tattling on your friends to their parents."

His head dropped forward until his brow rested on the steering wheel, hands white-knuckled on either side. I had a flashback of our trip to the make-out spot when he turned from that same position to smile at me. He turned now, but he wasn't smiling.

"You stupid, stupid kids." He spoke in a whisper. The second stupid was painfully drawn out.

"Zander!" I gasped.

"I need you to get out of my car now, Quigley." He said my name like he didn't know me.

"Zander?" Tears started. I didn't even know what I'd done.

"Get out, Quigley."

"But—"

"And don't bother telling Anne anything about Lance. He dodged a bullet. She's not good enough for him."

I opened the door slowly. Zander glared straight ahead.

"Please, Zander. Can we just—"

My words were cut off as the ignition sprang to life. My feet felt wobbly as I stepped onto my lawn.

"Zander?" I swiped at my running nose and swallowed a sob. "What about us?"

"I'm sorry, Quigley." He turned and gazed at me through his own wet eyes and slowly shook his head. "You're not good enough for me, either."

I stood watching his taillights disappear down my road. I waited long after he made the turn, sure he'd be back apologizing and begging to talk things through, shocked he'd left me standing in the street without even knowing if I even made it in safe. But he didn't turn around, and he didn't come back.

Chapter Thirteen

· · · · · · · · · · · · · · · · · · · ·

Sleeping in should feel more luxurious. Somehow, waking up to the harsh reality that the guy you thought might be your first real boyfriend hated you and your best friend's life tanked overnight took the pleasure out of waking sans alarm. Having claimed a stomach bug to explain my tearful return home in the middle of the night, I inadvertently excused my way right out of being able to hang with Anne and her mom after school.

I could handle one night home, but with so many questions about where I'd gone wrong with Zander swirling through my aching brain, a full day *and* night home alone felt claustrophobic. Way too much time to obsess about "what if"s.

I threw my books into my bag a little rougher than necessary. Whoever thought that school would turn out to be somewhere I'd escape to? It wasn't until I opened the door to the art room, late pass in hand, that I remembered that even here I had my share of problems.

Ten sets of eyes focused on me. I sighed in relief that David's weren't among them . . . until I heard the *click*. And another. I turned to the front of the class where David sat on my stool, smiling smugly at me and shifting his weight to make the uneven legs click. No one else was smiling.

I checked my watch, confused. Did I miss the class? This looked like everybody from Photography 101.

"Nice of you to join us, Quigley," Mrs. Albertt said.

"I have a pass," I said uneasily, and shifted my books into my other arm.

"That's fine. Go ahead and find a seat."

"But David's on my stool." I sounded like a whining kid.

"It seems we need to do a bit of shifting of responsibilities. I was just explaining to the class that due to your little mishap in the lab, they'd need to go out and reshoot their assignment."

Well, that explained the death glares. Sort of.

"I don't get it. Why? I thought they came out pretty well."

Mrs. Albertt raised one eyebrow. "Well, perhaps they might have before the damage. The destruction of everyone's work due to such carelessness is bad enough. I won't even go into the recklessness of smoking in a closed room full of chemicals. You're lucky all that happened was melted negatives and a few smoke- and water-damaged prints. Had you set off the main sprinkler system, you'd have destroyed the entire storeroom full of student work and be looking at far more serious consequences.

"It was a mistake on my part to have trusted an unsupervised student in the lab. You've had a long history of hard work in my classes, so I've decided not to bring this matter to higher authorities so close to graduation. However, you've proven that you're not responsible enough to be trusted with the position of teacher's assistant. I believe you owe your classmates an apology."

"What? I don't *smoke*! Cigarettes are nasty. Ask anybody— I've never smoked!"

Click. Click. Click. David sat in front, shaking his head in disapproval.

"Ask David! He was here with me. There was no fire, no cigarettes."

"That's true, Mrs. Albertt. When I left, everything was just fine. Quigley had made some mistake with the developing and had to redo the prints. I had to get home to watch my sister, so I couldn't stay and help her fix it. But everything was fine . . . when I left."

So this is what it felt like under a bus. I realized too late I'd been outplayed in the game of revenge. Anne had warned me David cared about his image to a freakish degree, but I'd let the handful of nice moments we'd had hanging out alone lull me into thinking he could be a bigger person and accept my change of heart . . . and prom dates.

Mrs. Albertt nodded approvingly at her star witness. "And the lab was shut nice and tight and all locked up when I came in the morning—keys in your cubby, Quigley. Obviously something happened. I am glad you weren't hurt, although I wished you'd have admitted this right away. You've put us all in a tight spot. Those negatives were meant to be used for the class's submission in the citywide show. Now the class will have to make arrangements to reshoot the project before the due date."

The groans around me held a thinly veiled undertone of hostility. Not good. "I truly don't know what happened, Mrs. Albertt, but I'm happy to help out as much as possible to make sure everybody gets their entry completed."

Mrs. Albertt smiled tightly. "I'm afraid I don't have the luxury of taking any chances, Quigley. David has offered to take over the teacher's assistant position for the rest of the semester. You can take a seat and complete the course as a student. Let's consider this matter closed and move on, shall we?"

I willed myself not to breathe until I could hide behind my textbook, out of David's sight. Tears would only add to my humiliation.

· · · · · · · · · · · ·

The sea of happy cafeteria munchers did little to improve my mood. I snagged a tray and defiantly asked the attendant for extra cheese sauce on my broccoli. Betterment Plan. Snort. That wasn't me—that was all Anne. I'd spent seventeen years perfectly content being me, making my own choices, making decisions based on my priorities—not anyone else's—and for what? To get pulled this way and that by everyone who flitted into my life, and blow it all when it really mattered?

This was the real deal—game time, baby. I smacked a fork next to the teetering plate of cheesy vegetables. It was like Ms. Parisi had said at the last design class—measure twice, cut once. The choices I had to make about the future would change the rest of my life. And here I was spending all my energy cleaning up after my best friend's craziness, getting so sucked in to one guy I couldn't see straight, and trying to save the feelings of another guy who, after a single unasked-for kiss, I'd blindly forgotten had only ever treated me like trash.

Anne would be off enjoying her Sex Week at some Ivy League school; Zander's heartless dismissal had ended any chance we had of something lasting; and Art Institute–declining David had basically accused me of trying to burn down the school. So after all I'd done, I'd be left here alone, begging for my job at the pizza factory back, hoping to make minimum wage. I swiped the last Diet Coke off the shelf next to the register, twisted the top off, and glugged. Yep. I had some measuring to do. And heck if there wouldn't be some people getting cut out of my life.

I slammed the bottle down without thinking, or putting the cap back on. A massive geyser of frothy brown liquid shot up and all over me. A slow round of applause began to build across the room, punctuated by giggles and pointing fingers. Usually reserved for the crash of dropped trays and broken dishes, I knew it was customary to acknowledge the clapping with a goofy "Oh my, doofus me" face, and maybe a fake curtsy or deep bow thrown in for style, but I just didn't have it in me. The soda drizzled in streams from my hair, which

I let fall over my face to cover my tears. I grabbed a handful of napkins and crouched down, pretending to mop off my soaked legs.

Through my bleary eyes, a pair of military boots clunked into view. I took the offered towel from his hand and glanced up past the I'D KILL FOR A NOBEL PEACE PRIZE to meet T-Shirt's concerned gaze. He bent down and picked up my backpack, flicking pools of bubbles off the straps before he slung it over one shoulder.

"Come on, I've got extra shirts in my locker."

It was about the only thing anyone could have said in that moment to make me smile. I didn't quite make it to smiling, but I gratefully let him lead me from the cafeteria. With a protective arm around my back, he walked between the crowd and me, concealing my red eyes and glaring down anyone who dared to snicker. I sighed and added another name to my list of people I'd judged too quickly.

We entered the hall and he gave me a little pat before dropping his arm.

"How's Anne?" he asked.

"I don't know. I didn't want to wake her and we didn't get to talk last night."

"Yeah, I thought I saw you there."

He waved at a passing group of sophomores wearing nun habits. Budding method actors trying to get into character, or just trying to draw attention to feed their egos, which Anne claimed was integral to being an actor. Not that she was biased.

"Just tell her I'm sorry, okay? I get it—we're done. But I really do feel bad about how it all went down," he said.

"What exactly did 'go down'?" I asked.

"First of all, she wasn't even supposed to be there. We agreed she'd do the preliminary and then stay out of the rest of"—he glanced around and lowered his voice—"the *deed*."

I thought back to that stupid half ruler, and the even stupider plan for revenge.

"So it *was* the light bar."

"Shhh. Look, all they know is that it's gone, and I hope for all of our sakes that's all they'll ever know. I can't believe she told you."

He shook his head, spun his locker combo, and yanked twice before a quick shoulder slam unjammed the metal door. He rifled through his things, finally pulling out a handful of shirts.

"Thanks," I said, flipping through for the least offensive one.

"No problem. I keep a bunch here in case I go right to the theater or somewhere after school. It's my remote closet. So last night, Anne calls out of nowhere, saying she wants to be in on the plan. When I picked her up, she was wired, and I could tell something bad went down, so I told her, 'No way.' Loose cannons aren't a safe bet, you know? But she was really raging over some deal with her mom, and believe me, I know how that can be. I thought it'd be a good distraction for her. But I didn't let her out of the car."

I handed I DIDN'T CLIMB TO THE TOP OF THE FOOD CHAIN TO BECOME A VEGETARIAN back and debated between the final two. YOU NONCONFORMISTS, YOU'RE ALL ALIKE lost out to HE WHO LAUGHS LAST, THINKS SLOW-EST, which even I had to admit was clever.

T-Shirt nodded his approval. "Philosopher chick, huh?"

"So why were you guys picked up?"

"The plan was going perfectly. One of the guys tracked the cop over the last week and saw he always hit Dunkin' Donuts for dinner. It was too classic not to go for, right? So I had Anne park my car around the corner, and the guys parked their van in back of the shop. Once the cop was elbow deep in his flatbread and cruller, we snatched the bar. They ditched it in the van, I ran back to Anne, and we got out of there. The guys sped off to deposit the goods in an undisclosed location and that should have been that."

"I can't believe you guys. What if the cop came out when your friends were putting it in the van?"

"They could have just driven off. I mean, the guy was missing his lights and siren, how fast could he have really chased anybody? I wish I could have seen his face! Problem was, someone saw me as I left."

"They ID'd you?"

"My shirt. Some woman pointed out my HANDBASKET shirt to her husband on their way into the shop. When the cop figured out what happened and asked for witnesses with any information, she mentioned it."

"Not much to go on, how did they even catch up with you?"

"That night when he first hassled us with all the car violations and the curfew ticket, I had my STOP FOLLOWING ME, I'M NOT A SHOPLIFTER shirt on. I guess it stuck in his head, so he thought of me. The cops looked up my tickets, put out an APB on my license plate, and there we were, hanging out with the po-po on an otherwise lovely Thursday night. All thanks to my signature expressions designed to make the world a happier place."

"Wow." On so many levels, wow.

"Tragic. Brought down by my own genius."

I was relieved Anne might legally have an easy out, but worried that my friend had ended up in such a dark place over her dad that committing a felony with T-Shirt and company seemed like a good way to kill an evening.

"Thanks for the shirt—I'll get it back to you."

"No worries, keep it. I never wear them more than once anyway, you know, in public. Gotta keep it fresh for the fans."

Anne wasn't kidding when she said T-Shirt's dad was loaded. I guess being the head of a hospital means your kid can pull off a disposable-clothing allowance.

"Quigley—thank goodness. I was so worried when you weren't in class!"

The sinking feeling hit the minute I recognized Mrs. Desmond's voice. It was Friday.

"The essay," I said.

"The essay! I can't wait to read it. The judges are expecting me to turn it in by three," she said. "I'm so glad this all worked out. This will really help you turn things around."

I opened my mouth, but no words came.

"Sorry, Mrs. D." T-Shirt reached into his locker. "I was

supposed to print it out for Quigley last night, and I spaced. Maybe you could give her a pass to hit the media center next hour?" He plunked his laptop into my hands.

"Nothing like cutting it to the wire, Quigley," Mrs. Desmond laughed. "Right down to the seventh hour." She scribbled out a slip excusing me from my next class. "Or sixth, as it were."

"Thanks," I stammered.

"No prob," T-Shirt said at the same time as Mrs. Desmond's, "You're welcome"

She gave him a questioning look and then smiled and headed on toward her class.

"Laters, Quigley," said T-Shirt. "You can drop my Mac off at the theater later. And just so you know, anything in there of questionable nature must be spam. Got it?"

"Got it," I mumbled, stunned by his save and the fact that I had to write a whole essay in an hour. He flipped my backpack over my still-damp shoulder and left me to wander down the hall trying to protect the expensive computer and fresh shirt from getting into the sticky mess. Not to mention, myself.

Chapter Fourteen

• • • • • • • • • • • • • • • • • • • •

"So you're okay?" I asked Anne. I could hear someone getting a rose or being voted off the island or kicked out of the sorority house or something in the background.

"Yeah. Sorry I wasn't up to talking last night. It was all just kind of overwhelming," she said.

"You think?"

"Did you tell her?" Ms. Parisi's voice called over the reality marathon.

"Oh, right. So Mom had this out-of-town show next weekend. She was going to fly out Saturday and be back Sunday, and just see about me crashing with you while she was away. But now, with me being jailbait or a flight risk or whatever—" Ms. Parisi's protests rang out over the commercials. "*Sooorrry*, I realize it's not a joke, but this is just Quigley. Anyway, she decided *it wouldn't give the right impression* to be leaving me alone right now."

"Really? From what T-Shirt said, you should be pretty much in the clear."

"He was at school today?"

"Yep. And get this, he loaned me his laptop to whip up that extra-credit essay I completely spaced. I don't even remember what I wrote—I just rambled for two pages."

"Nice one," said Anne. "We're hoping it all blows over, but one of those idiots took a movie on their cell and put it online. Mom's PR rep told her the pics those guys snapped as we were leaving the station made it online, too. But nobody seems to have picked up the story, probably because there isn't much to tell. I have a feeling the cops don't exactly want to advertise that one of their own got duped while chowing down a chocolate frosted, at least not until they come up with some evidence. The whole thing was crazy stupid, though—that thing with my dad put me over the edge. Not that I wasn't teetering on it anyway. Mom and I talked a lot about Dad today. I think I'm a little better now—I'm sorry you had to deal with my mess."

"I'm just glad you're okay," I said. It was impossible to stay mad at Anne.

"Thanks. But you don't sound like *you* are. What's up?"

"Nothing." I thought about Zander. And David. And my life in general. "Everything."

"What's going on?"

"Zander and I had a huge fight." I swallowed hard and tried to sound like I wasn't about to throw myself across my bed sobbing. "It's over."

"Come on, Quigley. I might have missed it at first, but that guy's crazy about you. No way it's as bad as you think. You probably just misinterpreted what he said."

"He said I'm not good enough for him."

There was a long pause.

"If I wasn't sort of on probation for something I sort of didn't do, I'd go over there right now and kick his crappy-drawing, MGB-driving, little—" A muffled voice stopped her. She pulled the phone away from her mouth. "Mom, he said she wasn't good enough for him."

I pressed my ear to the phone trying to catch any possible words of wisdom from Ms. Parisi. Anne came back translating the advice. "Mom says she knows Zander. There's no way he would say something like that and mean it. There must have been some major misunderstanding. She says to let him cool off and he'll come back apologizing like the gentleman that he is. That whatever it was probably had nothing to do with you." She held the phone away for a minute and came back parroting more. "She says that people say and do incredibly stupid things when they are upset about something completely unrela— Hey!"

I heard a good-natured swatting fight across the line and smiled. "I guess." I wasn't convinced I even wanted to be with someone who had it in him to talk to me that way. But it did make me feel a little better, hearing someone else say that it probably wasn't personal.

"Boys-schmoys. Here's something to cheer you up. I called because Mom wanted to invite you to come with us to her show, and she got us to tickets to some big Monet exhibit. Not my thing, but she thought you'd dig it."

"Rembrandt, you mean. Awesome. The one at the Met?"

She checked with Ms. Parisi. "Nope, Monet."

"But the only Monet exhibit right now is in Chicago."

"*I know!*"

I jumped up, squealing into the phone, knowing Anne was doing the same across town.

"Ohmigodohmigod! Are you serious?"

"Dead. She's going to call your folks and get the okay. We get to stay at this totally cute little boutique hotel right near The Magnificent Mile, hang backstage at the show, maybe even meet somebody cool—a bunch of celebs come to these things—and then tour the Art Institute. She said she wanted to thank us for all of our hard work in her class."

"Considering it looks pretty unlikely I'll be using the money for anything fun now, I guess that's not a bad consolation prize."

"I forgot about prom. It's still three weeks away. Maybe things will blow over? Look at me, I'm totally single, and I still have faith I'll snag a date from somewhere."

"I have faith that you will, too," I laughed. "But what about The Spikester?"

"I don't know." She lowered her voice. "Mom doesn't seem so keen on him. She's been pretty cool through all of this mess, so I thought I'd throw her a bone and let that one fizzle."

Hearing the shift in Anne and her mom's relationship almost tempted me to talk with my own folks about recent events, but the risk of their saying no to the Chicago trip on principle was too big a gamble. For now.

"I'm gonna go cheer myself up and pack for next weekend."

"Okay. Don't forget, we've got the Earth Day parade in the morning. Laters, Quigley!"

I groaned. "Great. Laters."

I hung up the phone gently. Anne sounded so good. It was like she had found her way back from the craziness that had been building the past year, without losing her focus and the person, for better or worse, that she was. I lay back on my bed and tried not to be jealous.

· · · · · · · · · · ·

The unseasonably warm Saturday morning had brought tourists into the old-town section of Providence. The parade route would pass along the cobblestone streets, ending at the river. The Earth Day Parade King would kick off the summer-season art installation by lighting seventeen bonfires that would reflect off the river's shimmering waters.

"I have a bad feeling about this," I said for the fourteenth time since we'd hopped off the city bus.

"It's fine. Just be glad we found someone who would let you borrow their instrument. 'Woodwind rental' isn't exactly in the budget."

"What if they ask me to play something?"

"I told you, it's not like that. There's no audition. They would have sent music for you to learn, wouldn't they? I think it just goes with the wood sprite, fairy, elfin vibe. Kind of like those panpipes you always see in the picture of the half-goat/half-man creature—but who would have panpipes?—so they asked for a piccolo."

We shuffled through the already-crowded blocks. People had placed blankets and lawn chairs along the sidewalks at daybreak to ensure a good viewing spot. The parade wouldn't even start for another thirty minutes, and people were giving us nasty looks for cutting through their staked-out territory. A live band started a rousing mash-up of "Wonderful World" and "It's Not Easy Being Green."

"What's the address, again?" I yelled over a team of bagpipers tuning up.

"We're looking for forty-two!"

"Isn't that forty-two on the corner?"

"Yep!" Anne grabbed my hand and pulled me toward a massive glass window filled with giant foam creatures of every shape and color, all covered in glossy swirls of paint.

"Wow—these are incredible!"

"This must be the guy's studio. They said to come and suit up here first. We'll meet the float on the next block!"

We stopped for a minute at the window to admire the

gorgeous blue-and-purple two-headed octopus-lizard inside. Behind it was an eight-foot-tall ear of corn with green leafy arms, a snaggletooth smirk, and eyebrows made of jet-black foam crows. A large burgundy eggplant with fangs grinned at passersby. Along the ground lay an assortment of giant ruby-red lobster claws and green foam talons with purple faux nails extending out a good eighteen inches. Two giant bare feet looked like they came off a dismembered troll in desperate need of a pedicure, complete with orange hair sprouting from the ankles.

"What is this place?" I asked.

A large teal sluglike creature waddled out the door toward us. It stood a head taller than me, had a fat tail that slithered behind it by eight feet, and fifteen to twenty large cat-shaped eyes springing from the top of its head. I jumped as one popped up to reveal a smiling face below.

"Hi, are you Anne and Quigley?" it asked.

Anne and I froze and looked at each other.

"Okay, the silent types. Well, I'm hoping you are my missing crew since everyone else is here and we're almost ready to begin."

"Hi, I'm Anne; this is Quigley."

I tried not to stare at what appeared to be a swimmer's cap on the guy's head, painted to precisely match the other foam eyeballs. I jumped as a series of long, pointy hackles sprang up from the creature's back.

"Great. Anne, you can head right inside since you'll need the bathroom to change. Quigley, you come with me."

Anne had scooted in without a word, as unnerved as I was by standing on the corner chatting with a large slug. I followed the blob of a guy, grateful the realistically shaped, though wildly painted, costume didn't include a corresponding slime trail.

"Oh, wait. Is there somewhere I should leave my piccolo case?"

The slug turned around and looked me up and down like *I* was the unhinged one. "Come again?"

"My piccolo case. I j-just need my piccolo, not the case," I stammered.

"You *need your piccolo*?"

"Don't I?"

"My God, where are they getting the extras these days," he whispered under his breath before turning with a big fake smile and speaking slowly, "Yes, dear. I suppose if you need your piccolo, you need your piccolo. Just come along." His hackles quivered back and forth in annoyance.

I jogged to keep up as the crowd made a wide berth for the slug before immediately crushing back closed, forcing me to step up and over while trying to keep the many swirling eyes on stalks in sight through the balloons and raised cones of cotton candy and cinnamon almonds. Suddenly, the masses parted as we passed the official starting line of the parade.

"Here, we are," the slug swept his tail around, nearly taking out several small children sitting on the curb, and motioned to a massive fairy tree house float.

"It's gorgeous," I said.

"Not completely certifiable then," he said. "Good."

Two small mushrooms suddenly popped up from the floor of the float and scurried over.

"She's here! You're walking with us!"

"Ah yes, meet the Fungus Among-us," said the slug, by way of introduction.

"Hi," I said, wondering if they were children inside the foam creations, and hoping they weren't expecting me to play them a tune to dance to during the parade.

"You need to step right into the trunk, no time to dilly-dally," said the slug.

"Excuse me?"

"Why—did you do something rude?" He shrugged at my blank look. "Sorry, old joke."

"This float is amazing. But am I supposed to spend the whole parade sitting inside the tree?" The little mushrooms twirled around me.

"Quigley, check it out!" Anne practically spun on air down the street, parting the crowd easily, and no wonder. Her clear, sequined bodysuit sparkled in an extremely flattering not-there way, and fit like a glove, despite the bulky middle bracket for a flight harness. The Vegas-esque getup featured The Spikester's unmistakable perfectly fitted touch.

"Wow, am I wearing that, too?" I asked with an equal measure of longing and fear. We watched as an intense griffin creature, previously hidden behind the trunk of the float's tree, reached down and easily lifted Anne to her perch in one of the fairy tree limbs. His talons peeled back as he clipped a thick metal guideline to her costume.

"Of course not, you're a puppeteer," said the slug.

"I am?"

"Don't worry, the costume doesn't have any of the fun, though challenging additions the rest of us have." His hackles sprang back up on command, as he revealed a string lever attached to his index finger. "But it was the artist's first creation, and we never have a showing without it. Didn't they tell you anything? We never allow 'the Scooby-Doo reveal' in this company. Our little theatrical surprises are the artist's statement that one should leave behind expectations of what should be and open oneself up to appreciate all the surprising and wonderful layers life offers."

The eggplant who'd just arrived stepped forward and reached across and gripped the corner of his fang-filled mouth to demonstrate. Instead of the grinning puppeteer I'd expected, three spring-filled snakes jumped out at me, leaving behind what appeared to be a weathered foam egg. Crack lines appeared before the top of the shell popped up to reveal a baby triceratops head with very humanlike eyes, one of which winked at me. "Most people wear more than one mask," the triceratops commented.

"Okay, somebody help Lenny get his snakes back in his mouth!" The slug turned back to me. "So anywho, you must change within the trunk. The boss traveled to the Bowl parade in California with half the cast, but we need to maintain his professional and artistic standards, especially on our home turf."

I looked up at Anne's tinkling laugh of delight as she delicately spun around a thick, ropy, foam-flower-covered vine, reveling in her own beauty. As usual, she floated above the insanity she'd pulled us both into.

"So wait. What do I have to do?" I asked. "I thought I was coming to play the piccolo."

"No." The slug's googly eyestalks shook back and forth impatiently. "You were coming to play the pic—" He broke out in laughter abruptly midsentence.

As the mushrooms, griffin, eggplant, and various other woodland and agriculture-based creatures joined in, I suddenly could relate to Alice, post–rabbit hole.

"Oh, my." The slug's jiggly eyes finally stilled as he gained control of himself. "I'm afraid you *are* in a pickle."

Which set them all off again.

· · · · · · · · · · · ·

Anne spent the parade alternating between twirling and flipping her fabulous self around the greenery of her elfin home, and mournfully mouthing, "I'm sooooo, sooooo sorry," down to me, in my giant seven-foot-high green-foam-pickle prison.

The first block, I concentrated on counting all the ways Anne owed me, while blinking the sweat out of my eyes, breathing by sipping air from the vent below and shuffling my giant troll feet, complete with purple hairy toes—in a way that didn't result in falling flat on my Vlassic.

The second block, I got my dill on and shook it a bit to the pounding bass of the band we followed, and stayed upright. Rather than feeling tempted to kick the little mushrooms playing ring-around-the-rosy around my bumpy green body, I spun inside their circle the opposite direction until they peeled off, dizzy at the contrast.

By the third block, the eight-foot-tall corn, slug, griffin, eggplant, and I were stealing the show from the beauteous acrobatic elves and earning loud cheers from the onlookers as we attempted a grotesque plant-animal-mineral version of the Rockettes' moves as the band began Sinatra's "New York, New York."

It was right about then that I saw T-Shirt on the sidelines. I glanced up, but Anne was otherwise engaged, posing for a group of culinary students from Johnson and Wales still wearing their white jackets and houndstooth-checked pants. He yelled to get Anne's attention, having worn a HOBBITS

ARE TOLKIEN MINORITIES cotton tribute to her appearance. She spun around at his voice and stared down at him for a long minute, before deliberately turning her back to him.

Her chilly body language would have been enough to relieve me of the hundred-plus-degree pressure cooker my costume had become, but T-Shirt looked like he'd been punched in the gut. As he turned away, I caught sight of David behind him, locked lip to lip with Maria. David's lips might have been firmly attached, but his attention was on the float, clearly trying to ensure that I got my intended punishment for daring to cross him. Loser.

I thanked the gods of all things pickled for the cover my costume provided, and strode forward to do a little do-si-do with the slug, cool as a cucumber with well-preserved pride.

Chapter Fifteen

● ● ● ● ● ● ● ● ● ● ● ● ● ● ● ● ● ● ● ●

Anne and Ms. Parisi did an admirable job ignoring the stares and whispers of the other passengers boarding the plane. After the past few days, they were probably so thrilled to be getting out of town they didn't even mind.

Although the police didn't have any more evidence to continue their investigation, the paparazzi had sunk their teeth in after the viral video tsunami spread across the country. Even late-night TV show hosts were making cracks about what they termed a Simpsonian "D'oh" moment. The last time Anne and I looked it up, the cell phone–captured clip of the cop leaving the entrance to the donut shop, and stopping slack jawed as the guys snuck unseen around the side toting his light bar, had been viewed over twelve million times.

After their police station clickfest, one of the reporters had used his slimy ways to get ahold of an illegally obtained police report and verified Anne's connection as a suspect.

Thankfully, my face was in shadows, but a clear shot of the two beautiful faces of the Parisis—Anne, defiant, and Ms. Parisi, distraught—made for ideal tabloid fodder.

There had been no formal charges tying Anne to the crime, but, despite her being underage, unscrupulous Hollywood talk shows spent long hours gossiping about what a shame it was for the formerly perfect Victoria Parisi to be so humiliated by her daughter. The vultures even speculated on what sort of mother she must be.

I sunk into the soft leather of my cushy window seat and tried to put it out of my head, like Anne and her mom seemed to be doing. Ms. Parisi might be used to getting bumped up on flights, but I had never ridden in first class before. I checked to see if anyone was looking and tucked the complimentary amenities bag full of tiny toiletries, socks, and a lavender-scented eye mask into my backpack for back at home, when I could savor it.

Finally, the line of boarding passengers slowed to a trickle. A flight attendant followed them, stopping at our aisle holding a tray of champagne glasses.

"Refreshment?"

"Oh please, yes," Ms. Parisi said, showing the first crack

in her poise as she gratefully accepted the glass and took a long deep drink.

"Thank you. Yes, me, too," Anne said with a smirk, but flashed an apologetic smile at her mom before correcting, "I'll have a Diet Coke, though."

"Me, too," I said, and flipped on the seat's lumbar massage feature. "Ahhh, this is what I needed last weekend after that parade."

"Awww, you were cuke," Anne said. "Seriously, you were a hit. I heard the slug asking if you'd be up for another show in the future. And I got to blow off T-Shirt and you got to blow off Zander. Perfect day!"

"What? Where was Zander?"

"You didn't— Sorry, I thought you saw him and iced him because of what he said."

"I didn't even see him. Who was he there with?"

"A few little kids in wheelchairs—they were in the handicapped section up front. He was with some redhead chick, but don't worry, they weren't acting like anything special. Does he have a sister?"

"I guess. I don't really know that much about his family. He never talks about them. Great, he probably thinks I blew him off. And while he was doing charity work of all things."

It didn't surprise me in the slightest that Zander would volunteer to take sick kids to a parade.

"You were more than a little incognito. And so what if he did. What he said was awful."

"Yeah, I guess."

"All set, Ms. Parisi?" asked the flight attendant, accepting her empty glass and offering a downy blanket.

"Thank you."

The attendant nodded and then placed a hand on Ms. Parisi's shoulder with a sympathetic smile. "How about I close this curtain."

We all glanced back at the dozen or so eyes gawking up at the Parisis.

"That would be lovely," said Ms. Parisi, and reached across the aisle to give Anne's hand a squeeze of support.

· · · · · · · · · · · · ·

Anne and I settled into our front-row seats. The giant tent buzzed with chatter and excitement, and the white runway gleamed like a mirror. A heavy, rhythmic thumping of nondescript music with an overtone of seductive jazz sax filled the venue as the lights dimmed.

"That's weird," Anne whispered. "She's usually more of a light, melodic type. Wonder if somebody on the soundboard screwed up."

I glanced over as a critic sitting next to me scribbled "bold departure" on his pad. Anne pointed out the recognizable fashion writers, and I spotted a sprinkling of celebrities in the masses.

Ms. Parisi strode out as a hush fell over the crowd.

"Thank you all for being here for a toast to Chicago's fashion history. As a designer, you never know when inspiration might hit and where it might come from. I think you'll notice a flash of spark and drive in this line not fully expressed in my usual designs. I hope you see this emergence of passion as the natural progression burgeoning from the classic roots and stately stalks of past collections—a vision inspired by someone I greatly admire—my daughter."

Ms. Parisi turned and strode back up the runway, throwing a kiss and wink at Anne as she passed.

The sax swelled as model after model, poured into slinky flapper-inspired gowns, kept in check by Ms. Parisi's signature highly constructed style clicked past us. Heads held high, exuding everything from coy flirtation to smoldering sensuality, they pranced past, drawing spontaneous bursts of applause and exclamations from the enchanted crowd.

"It's *so* you, Anne," I said.

Anne beamed and jumped up with the rest of the crowd for a thundering finale as the entire line of models entered the runway for a final pose. Ms. Parisi followed them, graciously accepting the renewed cheers. She paused alongside us and reached one hand down for Anne. Anne tucked one heel onto her seat and stepped gracefully onto the runway— a move that would have induced blooper-style footage had I tried it—and walked arm in arm with her mom, laughing and waving. They stopped and stood, proud and brave at the end of the runway under a sea of flashes that were likely to be less about the fashions than the designer. They followed the line of models back through the curtains as the lights came up.

The audience pounced on their cell phones, abuzz with talk of the designs and the moment Ms. Parisi flaunted her support of her daughter. Anne's cheeks flamed as she happily weaved her way through the crowd to our seats, accepting compliments and good wishes from everyone she passed.

I hugged her tight.

"I can't even imagine what you're feeling right now."

"It just can't get any better than this, can it!"

I laughed. "Should we head back to the hotel now?"

"I kind of want to go find Mom. She got whisked off the second we passed the curtains. It's total chaos back there."

"Isn't that why she wanted us to just meet her back at The Talbott?"

Anne started shifting back through the seats toward the stage.

"Yeah, but who knew she was going to pull this! I just want to thank her. Come on, bring your camera. Shoot some of the flowers and champagne and half-naked model mania of a post–fashion runway show. Maybe you'll get your winning citywide contest shot!"

She had a point. I'd been carrying the school's loaner camera around my neck like an albatross, reminding me of the David mess and the fact that I hadn't replaced my own entry for the contest yet.

I followed her, snapping away as dresses whipped past me and shoes were flung across the lens to waiting assistants positioned next to tissue-paper-filled boxes. I got a nice photo of a model swiping one side of her dramatic makeup off through a magnifying mirror. I *click-click*ed until we reached her mom's dressing room and it hit me.

"Wait, Anne! I've got it. The perfect shot. I'll snap right as you open the door and catch her reaction and your mutual perfect, emotional, authentic moment! You just need to cheat toward me so I can get at least half your profile, maybe three-quarters, and still see her face. Just turn the knob with your arm wide so I can get a clear shot, and don't forget to look as happy and excited as you are right now."

We busted into giggles a few times and finally steadied ourselves for the "candid" shot.

"Okay. One, two—"

I brought the camera into focus and nodded. She threw open the door, and I heard the *click* as I snapped a picture worth millions, of three very shocked faces, two of which featured perfectly matching chin dimples.

• • • • • • • • • • • • • • • • •

Chapter Sixteen

Keith Gordon was the first to speak, though his eyes stayed glued on Anne's face. "I am so sorry, Victoria. You said she wouldn't be——"

"I know," Ms. Parisi said. "Anne? Are you okay?"

Anne nodded, staring at Keith Gordon.

"Quigley, would you——"

"Go? Sure, I'll go. Let me, I'll just——"

"No, sweetheart," Ms. Parisi said. "I was just going to ask you to step in and close the door. If it's okay with Anne?"

Anne nodded again. Her whole body was trembling. I nudged her forward a little so we could close the door behind us.

"Water?" My voice came out in a squeak.

Anne nodded. Ms. Parisi and I dove for the cooler, anxious to help in any small way. Keith Gordon seemed paralyzed in a half-seated lounging pose on the dressing table.

Anne glugged half the bottle down at once, nostrils flared as she tried to suck in air.

"Victoria, may I?" Keith asked.

Ms. Parisi sat down hard on the cooler. "Sure."

"Anne, I'm at a loss for words," he said. "I have the advantage here, I know. I planned the trip assuming I'd be seeing your mother, but I didn't realize you might . . . I'm sorry. There's just this mixed-up bundle of happy, ecstatic, pissed-off, sad, and about every other emotion you can think of hitting all at once right now."

Anne's nod was so slight he probably missed it.

"I want to grab you and hug you. I mean, my God! This is just . . . *amazing*! I mean, look at you! I don't know what to say. I'm scared as hell you're going to think I'm some nut you don't even know. Do I have any right to even be talking to you? From what your mom says, my suspicion was right. It's hard to swallow everything I lost—we lost—but you're just so . . ." He shrugged and swiped at tears that accompanied his joyful laugh.

My head spun from holding my breath. Anne still hadn't moved a muscle or said a word. Keith Gordon slid down into the dressing table chair with his head in his hands.

"God, I'm sorry; I'm just a mess. Since I saw that photo,

every minute of every day this past week, all I could think of is what I'd say, how I'd act—God, even what I'd wear! How stupid is that? You know how many times I changed my shirt this morning? Then I sweated right through that one and had to change again.

"And here I am, rambling on like an idiot, when I just wanted to make a good impression and maybe be somebody you might like or want to get to know or something. And there you were up there on that stage looking so beautiful, looking out so confidently with *my mother's eyes*, next to your mom, who is still every bit as beautiful as when we met almost two decades ago, both of you so full of life and strength—please, Anne. Help a guy out here, tell me what you're thinking."

Anne opened her mouth and shut it. With a little frown between her eyes she asked the golden question. "So, it's true?"

Mr. Gordon and Ms. Parisi looked to each other before nodding. Seeing the biggest superstar in the world so hopeful, practically begging for acceptance, I worried the old Anne would resurface and cut him to shreds. Instead, her expression softened into an emotion I never thought I'd see on my best friend's face. It took a minute to recognize it. She was shy.

"So, you're . . . happy?" she asked. "About me?"

Mr. Gordon's hands were clenched together so tight his knuckles went white. His head bobbed up and down like one of those dashboard bobblehead dogs on steroids.

The long silence while she considered this was pure torture. "Cool," she said, and smiled.

Mr. Gordon rose and stepped forward, arms outstretched, and then stopped just short of hugging her. He looked to Ms. Parisi and back at Anne. "May I? Sorry—I'm just so nervous about doing the wrong thing."

Anne laughed and stepped forward into his hug. I raised my camera instinctively and caught their laughter and wonder with a *click*. Ms. Parisi stepped forward to join them, and I stepped back to capture another family moment and give them some space. More than a few tears were wiped away.

"I just knew it," Mr. Gordon said. "The minute I saw that picture on the news, I told my wife 'My God, I think that's my daughter.'"

Anne stiffened and pulled away. "Look. My mom's a great mom. She's done a great job. It's not her fault I screwed up and got into trouble. I don't need someone coming in trying to take me—"

"No, no. God, no. Anne—nothing like that would ever

happen," Mr. Gordon said. He looked to Ms. Parisi for backup.

"No, baby. Keith's not taking you anywhere. Nothing's changing at all."

Anne eyed the two warily.

"Anne, I have a lovely wife, who I do think you'd like. She also happens to be a big fan of your mom's, as an artist and a person. She loves design and was addicted to that reality show. Her complimenting your mom's style and compassion with the young people really opened the door for me to mention our past. And thank God I did. I've been shooting out of the country for the past four months. She was the one who e-mailed me the tabloid shot and encouraged me to come speak with Victoria. Oh! And you have a new baby sister."

He pulled out his wallet to show her pictures. Opposite the tiny little toddler with big brown eyes was the infamous Parisi police station photo, cropped so it looked like a regular headshot of Anne. "Or you could, if you wanted. I don't know. I guess she's not blood related, so there's no pressure for you to make room in your life for this crazy unexpected side of your extended family."

His eyes measured Anne's reaction, but she was still guarded. "Or even me, if that's not what you want," he added.

"Look, as much as I would have loved to raise you and see every little step you made growing up, you're already there. Anyone can see what a great job your mom did. It's your life, and I don't want to cause you any pain if you don't want to share it with me. We'd love for you and your mom to maybe come out for a visit. When you're ready. We have a big guesthouse. You could maybe bring your friend, too?"

They all suddenly remembered I was in the room.

"I'm sorry!" Anne said. "Mr. Gordon, this is my friend, Quigley."

"I know I just promised not to be pushy, and though I'd be tickled, I'm not saying you should, or would ever want to, call me 'Dad,' but *Mr. Gordon*? Please, at least 'Keith.' We can maybe see how things go from there?"

Anne nodded. Mr. Gordon stepped over to shake my hand. Without the "deadbeat" status hanging over him, he really was gorgeous.

"I'd love to dump this movie I'm shooting, and hang out with every picture album and old wrinkled report card you have, to relive every minute I missed. And I will, if that's what you want. But I have to be straight with you—"

"You don't want anyone to find out about me," Anne said with resignation.

"God, no. The opposite, actually. *You* might not want to have anyone find out about *me*. As glamorous as it all seems, I really don't have a normal life. You need to decide for yourself if that's the way you want to live. If it were my choice, I'd walk out right now screaming this amazing news to everyone. But outside those doors is a team of the fourteen well-trained professionals it took just to sneak me in here for a half hour.

"That's life for me, but it doesn't have to be life for you. I'm sorry that my reality requires this kind of decision for you—hey, maybe I'll blow this next film and make the flop of the century. Just to loosen up the pressure?"

He smiled, but it didn't reach his eyes. Ms. Parisi put her arm around Anne.

"I've apologized to Keith for not coming clean with him all those years ago. It's no excuse, but I wasn't much older than you girls are now. I truly tried to do the best thing for everyone. Some decisions are tougher than others, and making them too quickly cuts off your ability to see all your options. We still have a lot to talk over, but knowing where we were and where we planned to go at the time, he's chosen to forgive me. I just want you to know, our issues have nothing to do with how the two of you proceed from here."

Anne smiled and nodded. "I get it. Maybe it's best right now to keep things low key. Can we e-mail or talk on the phone, at least?"

"Absolutely. Come to think of it, I think my wife needs a whole new look. I can't think of a better designer for the job. Of course, that will mean spending quite a bit of time putting together a new wardrobe?"

"Well, with proper fittings, it really would be most convenient to come for an extended stay," said Ms. Parisi. "I think my schedule opens up right after graduation."

"Great! We're all set. I need to sneak back out of here before someone notices the extra security loitering about and starts getting nosy. Your mom's got my direct contact info, Anne." He pulled her into a last, long hug. "Nice to meet you, Quigley. When you come out to California, we'll have more time to talk, and you can fill me in on all the real dirt about my daughter's life."

The word *daughter* hung in the air, and from Anne's beaming face, it seemed our earlier claim that life didn't get any better had been very premature.

"Okay, guys—don't laugh." Keith stepped to the door and knocked three times before pulling a baseball cap low over his eyes, adding shades, and throwing the hood from his sweatshirt over the combo. A burly guy from earlier, who I'd assumed was a dresser for the models, opened the door and escorted Anne's dad away while talking in a low voice into a headset.

• • • • • • • • • • •

Crossing from the busy special exhibit hall, I dragged Anne toward the modern art wing. Ms. Parisi had left us to wander on our own while she used her influence to see about pulling some strings in the Art Institute's Admissions Department. Desperate times called for desperate measures, and considering I couldn't even remember what I had written in the motivational essay, I needed help if I was going to have any chance of getting into my dream school.

The long weekend lines masking the front of the buildings carried through into the Monet exhibit. Something just felt off. Maybe it was claustrophobia from the mass of tourists flooding the museum, CityPasses clutched tight in their hands, but the picture I'd been carrying in my head over the years didn't fit the reality.

"What are you looking for?" Anne asked as I pulled her into yet another room and back out.

"I'll know when I see it." I stopped short. A couple sat,

back to back, on a wide marble bench. Sketch pads balanced across their laps, they were lost in each other and the art surrounding them. The art was all wrong—large, graphic, modern abstracts. Nothing at all like the statues and figurines at home. But I found what I was missing. "I want that."

Anne looked around the room. "I think they might have prints in the gift shop."

"No, not the art. I want that. Them." My whispered words made no sense. I wanted what they had. What I had had and lost. The feeling overwhelmed me, and I swallowed past the lump in my throat.

"So get them," Anne whispered back.

"Huh?" I turned to see Anne holding out my camera. "You can't have a camera in here!"

"Well, I do. I tucked it in my bag just in case," she said. "You want them, go for it. Just don't use a flash."

"But these pieces are too modern. It would probably be a copyright violation."

"Do you want shots of the art?"

"No. But what about invasion of privacy?"

"Sometimes, if you really want something, you've just got to take your shot, Quigley."

Before I let myself think any more, I snatched the camera.

The girl stretched, and then let herself lean back into the guy. Her neck lolled intimately against his shoulder, and he leaned back to nuzzle her, still sketching. *Click.*

The sound echoed through the high-ceilinged hall, and the couple started.

"Sorry!" Anne called over her shoulder and grabbed my hand to pull me away toward the exit, giggling with exhilaration. "I sincerely hope you got it."

"I think I did," I said, and tucked the camera down inside my top, holding my jacket up to shield the large lump from being so noticeable.

Chapter Seventeen

. . . .

"So, it came out well?" Anne asked.

I shoved my books into my locker.

"Really, really well. I don't even care if I get into the show or not. I think it's my favorite piece."

"Wouldn't it be funny if it got into the show, and Foster Neuwirth walked up and it turned out to be one of *her* collages in the background?"

"Yeah, hilarious," I snorted. "I found a workaround that ended up making it even better. I used a technique I read about to smear the background while developing it. It made the couple really stand out, kind of like the whole world was swirling away because they were so into each other . . . and covered the contraband images."

The school announcements crackled through the speakers. "Good afternoon, students. We would like you to join us in congratulating senior Quigley Johnson, who has won the regional Rotary Club essay contest, and a one-hundred-dollar prize. Quigley will be reading her essay at the Annual Rhode Island State Rotary Club banquet dinner this Thursday evening, along with the state's other regional finalists, in the hopes of winning a five-thousand-dollar scholarship to the college of her choice. Thank you, Quigley, for doing our school proud."

"Oh my God, Quigley—you won! Did you know you might win a scholarship?"

People were clapping me on the back as they passed.

"No! Maybe Mrs. Desmond said something about it. I didn't pay attention because I didn't think there was any way I'd even come close."

"You're going to win, I just know it," Anne squealed.

"I don't even remember what I wrote. It was the day after I had that big fight with Zander."

"You never told me what started that whole mess."

I considered hiding the truth from Anne again, but now that things were cool with her dad, maybe it would be okay to be straight about it.

"It was about you, in a way."

"Me?"

"Not you, exactly. He wigged out about the collecting expeditions—just furious."

"Oh nooo! I'm so sorry, Quigley. I can't believe I was so stupid. But you didn't even have anything to do with that."

"It's fine. He found out I knew about the sign in your room and didn't tell your mom, and then he went completely berserk."

We walked toward the office to collect my prize.

"Did he really say you weren't good enough for him?"

All the excitement from the essay contest slipped away at the painful memory. "Yeah."

"Well, I'm truly sorry. If it makes you feel any better, that Friday night, after our reality marathon, I called T-Shirt and found out where the sign came from. Mom went with me and we put it back up. You should have seen her sneaking around, diving in the bushes when a car passed, then running back out and tightening each screw until it was back up, good as new."

Imagining the elegant Ms. Parisi decked in camo doing anti-vandalism made me smile.

"I'm glad," I said. "I felt weird when I saw the sign in your room, but I didn't want to say anything."

"Next time, do. I was being lame."

"Okay."

She stopped short of the office. Never a big fan of the administration, I knew her recent brush with trouble made her more leery of getting too close to the ones holding suspension passes. "Are you sure you're okay? You seem pretty down for a girl who just won a hundred bucks."

"Yeah. I just really miss Zander. The swirly effect from the print sparked a few other ideas and I started sketching, but every picture I drew kept leading me back to him. Talk about a tortured artist." I shrugged. "I made him a copy of the contest print for his birthday, not that I'll even get the chance to give it to him. Besides, even if I found a way to apologize or explain, I'm not sure we could find our way back to the way it was. He was pretty harsh."

"I don't blame you. But Zander is so . . . Zander. I'd hear him out. Maybe he'll be the one apologizing?"

"I guess we'll see Wednesday at class, if he shows this week. I'd better go get my check."

Anne hugged me. "Seriously, great job. Can I come to your dinner and hear the speech?"

"Only if you track down T-Shirt. He's been AWOL since the parade. I was in such a rush, I only printed off the copy of my speech I turned in. My speech is still on his laptop!"

"Okay, fine." Anne made a face. "I hope you see how much better of a friend I'm being now."

The secretary made me pose with a beaming Mrs.

Desmond, the principal, and the check, like it was one of those giant Publishers Clearing House awards. I gracefully accepted the fact that after four years of near anonymity, apart from a badly retouched headshot, it seemed I could no longer escape the notice of the yearbook editors.

• • • • • • • • • • • •

"It's Thursday morning, Anne. Twelve hours until impact. What am I going to do?"

I still didn't have a copy of the speech. T-Shirt's dad had sent him on a college-visit trip, probably to keep him out of town and away until the police mess died down. At best, all I could hope was the Rotary Club would have a copy for me to read from. Any time for practicing was long gone.

The other entrants probably memorized their pieces with a coach. Or practiced giving it to classes filled with students in preparation for the public-speaking stint. I knew I wasn't going to win, but I really didn't want to look like a complete fool while losing, or embarrass Mrs. Desmond, who seemed to really be pulling for me. I'd even confided in her about the developing-room disaster, and she'd promised to write a glowing letter of recommendation to offset the missing "teacher's assistant" credit to supplement my college applications. With no proof of what happened, I'd just have to trust in karma to take care of David's suspected role in the mess.

"Don't blame me, Quigley. I'm not the one making T-Shirt blow off school. I know you're bummed about Zander not showing again last night, but I'm sure it wasn't anything personal."

"This was the very last design class. I might never see him again. You don't think it's possible he ditched to avoid seeing me? 'Doctor's appointment' is the oldest excuse in the book and two weeks in a row is more than a little suspicious. Did The Spikester say anything?"

"No, but he was too wiped out for much in the way of conversation. Something about his kid having nightmares about gummy bears coming to life and chasing him into a sea of milk to steal his Honeycombs. I should start paying more attention so when I get to hang out with"—she paused and mouthed "my sister"—"I'll know what to do."

"Good plan. But it doesn't save me now."

"Wait. Aren't you heading to art class? Ask David. He can scoot over to T's house and get it for you from his laptop. Their families know each other, don't they?"

I laughed. "Sure. I'll just do that. Because doing favors for me is what David likes to do best."

Anne shrugged. "Maybe he's over it by now. Bat your eyes and make nice until you get the speech. He owes you—use the loser and then lose the user. What other choice do you have?"

I waved to her and entered the art room to the annoying *click-click-click* of my former stool. I plastered a sweet smile on my face and bit the bullet.

"David, do you think you could do me a favor?"

He snorted in reply.

"Please. It's just that T-Shirt has the only copy of my speech I have to give tonight on his laptop. He hasn't been in all week and I'm screwed if I don't have it to read."

"What's it worth to you?" he asked.

Mrs. Albertt walked in and flashed me a cheery smile. Very strange. I gave up on David and found my seat. I'd remained the class pariah since the reshoot/fire fiasco, which meant I had my own table to spread out on. This also meant no one was close enough for a high five when Mrs. Albertt made her announcement.

"We have a student of many talents in our midst," she said, and walked over to a covered easel in the corner. "I present you with this year's entry for the citywide art show . . . Voilà!"

I stared at the sketching couple, frozen in their intimate moment in time. The clicking of the stool stopped.

"Seriously?" I heard myself say aloud. David said something a little more colorful.

"Quigley, there was no question. The maturity of emotion shown through this piece, the technical ability, the nuance of effect you used within the development stage . . . it's simply exquisite. I'm so proud. I think you've finally found your focus."

On Mrs. Albertt's lead, the class offered a begrudging and brief round of halfhearted applause. David chose not to join in. The taste of revenge was sweet, even though it meant I could kiss any chance of getting my speech from T-Shirt good-bye.

· · · · · · · · · · · ·

Anne's phone rang on our way to the dinner. "Quigley, can you get that—I'm not allowed to talk while I'm driving."

"Good for you!"

Anne's return to mostly sane Anne had some perks. One was that her mom returned the use of the car to her as long as she kept up her responsible lifestyle. Another was that she was doing less than half the stupid things she used to do, so riding with her no longer served as the ultimate test of nerves.

"Hey—Anne's phone."

"Quigley?"

"David?"

I looked at Anne, who shrugged, her eyes still on the road.

"Yeah, I kind of erased your number, so T gave me Anne's. I figured you'd be together. I've got your speech."

"Really? I thought—"

"I know. I was just being a jerk. Do you want it or not?"

"Yes, that'd be awesome. Except we're already on the way to the dinner, and I don't think we can make it on time if we have to turn around."

"No worries, I'm already here. Mrs. Desmond told me where the banquet hall is. The speech is in a black folder, and I'm giving it to the chick in charge now—she's got a red suit jacket on. Cool?"

"Thank you so, so much!"

"Whatever. Have fun."

I tucked Anne's phone back in her purse. "You won't believe this, but David dropped off my speech. This is great, now I can just sit and relax during the dinner. There was never any way I was going to win this, but I feel better knowing Mrs. Desmond won't look bad."

We found our seats, but the woman in the red blazer was nowhere to be seen. She finally made her appearance at the podium in front of the packed room. I gave her a little wave and she nodded, lifting the black folder and miming that it was there and accounted for.

I turned to Anne. "So much for a read-through ahead of time."

"Don't worry, you'll be fine."

The woman tapped the microphone, and the din of voices and clinking glasses died down.

"Welcome to the Annual Rhode Island State Rotary Club banquet. As you know, we've invited the winning students from regional contests throughout the state to share their moving and motivational speeches with us this evening. But first, I'm afraid they'll have to bear with us as we get a little bit of business out of the way."

Anne pulled out a notebook and started a list of movies to rent for our anti-promapalooza party. Knowing we were ditching the dance together soothed any bitterness over the Betterment Plan going bust. I tuned out the attendance and munched on my salad, spreading the roll with a tiny butter sculpture that looked like a seashell. After today's news about the citywide contest, nothing could ruin my day.

"And our final bit of business is appropriate for the company we have this evening, allowing yet another deserving young person to jump-start his or her education with the help of a full year's tuition and expenses while he or she adjusts and makes new plans for the future. The third annual Alexander Macintosh III Scholarship for Injured Athletes applications have been narrowed to three—"

"Quigley, isn't that Zander's—"

"Yes," I hissed, looking around the dimly lit room for the familiar face I couldn't get out of my head. Maybe he was here to hand out some award from his family. It must be fate.

"—and Bucky 'Fastball' Bauers in Appleton, seventeen, tragically snared in a piece of machinery on his family's farm—which I would think might hold appeal, considering young Alexander's memorable feats on the mound."

"It must be a different Alexander," I whispered to Anne. "He's never said a word about baseball, or any sports, for that matter."

The woman to my left leaned in. "You should have seen our Alexander in his day. I remember the first time he was in the paper. Tiny little thing back then, not even ten, but what an arm! The Macintoshes have been in the Rotary for years and years, but even if he weren't one of our own, I'd like to think we'd still have taken notice. Those scouts sure did. They were circling like wolves from his freshman year. He might have planned to go on to school and play, but people say the big leagues would have called him straight onto a farm team or better."

"Farm team?"

"Where they groom the players to move up into major league baseball," the woman explained. "Some people even said he might have been called straight up to the big leagues. I don't know about that, though. That might just be the kind of romantic legend talk that happens after a bad accident. But no doubt, he'd have gotten there one day."

"Accident?"

"Ohhh, Quigley." Anne's ashen face as she held out her phone.

I grabbed it with a trembling hand, making out random phrases as I scrolled through her hastily pulled-up news story. "Foggy spring morning . . . broadsided . . . missing stop sign . . . driver pinned by truck entering the unfamiliar intersection without slowing."

The words registered, and blood pounded like a drum in my ears. I could have stopped at the story's title, "Star Pitcher Survives, Career Over Before It Starts." Ugly fat tears fell down my cheeks. It explained so much. Anne hugged her stomach before leaning her elbows on her knees, covering her face with her hands and giving in to her own guilt and shame at what her actions might have caused.

"We've tallied the member votes, and Bucky Bauers will indeed be this year's recipient. As tradition—and our Finance Committee—dictates, we have chosen to make one-thousand-dollar scholarships available to the two runners-up to help toward costs and what they have lost in athletic scholarships."

I rose from the table, looking for Zander's face in the crowd, and moved blindly toward the exit, dialing his number. Voice mail. I hit resend. Voice mail. Someone grabbed my arm as I passed. I looked up at the whole room staring at me.

"Ms. Johnson, you're up. Quigley will be offering her essay, 'Measure Twice, Cut Once.'"

A spotlight hit my face, and I put one arm up to shield my eyes from the light. Encouraging applause swelled in the room as five hundred expectant faces looked to me. I realized that reading the two-page piece would take a lot less time than trying to excuse my way out of the speech, and turned toward the stage.

I flipped open the folder and tried to focus on the title. I couldn't even look in Anne's direction, though I could tell she was still hunched over. I took a deep breath to steady my voice.

"Measure Twice, Cut Once," I said loudly into the microphone. I noticed a faint note of hysteria in my tone, but I wasn't stopping. "In life we must make choices. We must face challenges. The best way to overcome these challenges is to 'climb every mountain' to get the best view of our problems. We have to say, 'So long, farewell' to our insecurities."

I didn't remember a bit of it, but at least they couldn't tell that from my reading. Something felt off. I glanced further down the page. When had I ever used the word *byway* before? I pushed the niggling feeling away. I just wanted to be done and on my way to find Zander.

"Good grades, art, grabbing for brass rings—these top the list of 'my favorite things.' I say aloud, 'I have confidence' in me. It's as easy as 'do-re-mi—'"

It rhymed. What the hell was going on? This was not my speech. I faltered, looking up for red blazer lady. The massive crowd looked back at me expectantly. A few people called out encouragement, thinking I had a case of the nerves. I flipped the page, confused.

"When I was 'sixteen going on seventeen,' I often felt like a 'lonely goatherd—'"

Titters broke out, and it hit me where the vaguely familiar words came from—*The Sound of Music*. I stepped back and flipped to the final page, a bold and perfectly drawn Art King crown adorned the bottom. Something just snapped. I leaned into the microphone.

"You know what? High school is awful. *It's awful.*" I reveled in the slightly shocked faces, looking to each other for cues on how to respond. "I know that's not what parents want to hear, what you guys want to hear. But it's the truth. You spend half your energy trying not to get trashed by some jerk who doesn't like you, not because you ever really did anything to him, but because you are different from them and don't want what they do. Or not different—maybe you have a lot in common, but instead of seeing that as a good thing, they see you as competition and have to spend all their time tearing you to pieces to make sure they look better.

"The other half of the time you spend trying to fit in. Why? I don't know. Most of the people you are trying to fit in with aren't the people you would want to hang out with, anyway. It's the people you are afraid of who you spend most of your time trying to impress. Buying these jeans and that computer. Got to have those shoes and this purse. Got to get this cool job to afford those jeans and that purse. It's a never-ending cycle of wasted energy. And then the good people trickle past, and you blow it. Because you're too busy playing some stupid image game to remember to show your real self.

"Maybe, if we spent a little less time on all that useless drama, we would have enough time to do what our real jobs are—making big decisions wisely. Personally, I think it's pretty insane to ask anybody my age to be wise when our heads are spinning in fifteen different directions. Maybe making big decisions wisely is just a matter of measure twice, cut once."

I grabbed the microphone from the holder and strolled as I spoke, arm flung out at some invisible place outside the hall.

"*Measure twice, cut once.* I really want to go to the Art Institute of Chicago. But why? Because I've always wanted to? Is that as good as I can do? Because it sounded cool to me when I was twelve and it's easier to just go with the flow? I never gave it a second thought. It was my first thought, and I didn't have the energy to take a second look and find out if it still fits.

"Measure twice, cut once. I don't tell my friend what she's doing is stupid and dangerous—sorry, Anne. Why? Am I unsure whether it is stupid and dangerous? No, I just don't want to rock the boat or cause her any more stress when she's going through a tough family time. Maybe if I gave it a little more thought before deciding to keep my mouth shut, I'd see that the stress she'd have if things went bad could totally wreck her family and her life. And on top of that, what she's doing could ruin someone else's life!

"Do you think those kids who stole the stop sign at Zander's intersection ever gave a second thought as to what might happen after their prank? I don't think so. I know they didn't. Because I go to school with those guys. Maybe not the exact ones who took that exact traffic sign, but they might as well be. None of them want to hurt anybody. They just never gave it a second thought.

"I know big decisions aren't going away, and that learning to make those choices is part of growing up. But maybe learning to stop and give things a second measure should be just as important, before we cut our way into a consequence we just can't live with."

I clunked the microphone in its stand and left the podium, walking straight out to the parking lot, hitting resend again and again, not caring if Zander thought I was a crazy stalker chick. An echoing roar of applause erupted from the building a few minutes later. Probably for my having left. Anne ran out. We hugged and got into the car.

"Are you okay to drive?" I asked.

She nodded. "Are you okay?"

"Yeah. Sorry, I guess I sounded like a nut in there. It was all just too much. No wonder he never talks about his past."

"I get it. And you didn't sound like a nut to everybody. After you left, some guy walked up to the podium and handed something to the red blazer lady."

"Let me guess—a note suggesting they do a background check on prospective speakers before handing them a mic?"

"No. It was a check made out to the Alexander Macintosh III Scholarship fund—to cover the full tuition and expenses of the other two finalists."

I stared at Anne.

"What? Not just because of my stupid speech. Who on earth would do such a thing?"

"T-Shirt's dad."

Chapter Eighteen

· · · · · · · · · · · · · · · · · · · ·

I had worked all night to finish the gift, but the end effect was worth it. I didn't have the loaner camera anymore, so I took photographs from old shoots and morphed the focal point to leave a blank still spot of photo paper canvas in the middle of chaotic movement. I went back in my head to Ms. Parisi's first class. Using long fluid lines, I sketched a fiery purple-and-red reproduction of Zander's dress on a faceless model standing on top of a table in the busy school cafeteria.

The furry mohair couture appeared perched on a traffic island between lines of speeding cars. The Daughters of the American Revolution garden party dress donned a willowy figure riding a single falling leaf down from the branches of a sugar maple. Soon, I had a full portfolio done. I wrapped it and left the now framed print of the sketching couple loose on top. That one would come later.

· · · · · · · · · · · ·

I walked up the hospital corridor to the physical therapy wing, preparing myself to be turned away, or worse. Anne came through when she reached out to The Spikester for the details on Zander's whereabouts. In my desperation to see Zander face-to-face, I had jumped at The Spikester's suggestion to show up and surprise Zander but was questioning it with every step down the waxed floor.

A nurse walked me in and pointed out Zander, who was zoned out between reps while sitting on a piece of equipment that could cross as a workout machine or torture device. In the corner, the redhead Anne described from the parade helped a little boy lean on crutches and shift one ankle at a time down on a padded floor mat.

I averted my eyes as I came around the front of the therapy machine and realized Zander sat shirtless. I blushed dark red at the sight, half in awe of his well-defined and sweaty body, half in shock at the mass of swirling pearly-white scars thickly winding around his left shoulder and extending down like badly sewn seams. In the full minute it took him to register my face, I had to stop myself from sprinting out three times, longing for the safety of my car. Zander self-consciously jumped for a towel to cover his scars, then shrugged with a sigh of defeat and looked up at me, eyes hopeful for acceptance.

"Hi," he said softly. He struggled his way out of the machine and stretched. He led me out into the hall, pulling on a T-shirt.

"Sorry, I didn't mean to bother you. It's okay, I'll go."

"No, no. Just wanted to talk and not disturb Brett—" He pointed back toward the room at the boy leaning heavily into his crutches. "I help with him sometimes. He's kind of like a little brother."

"Anne said she saw you at the parade. I was the pickle."

He raised one eyebrow, and I giggled in relief of the familiar Zanderness of him.

"It's kind of a long story," I said.

We stood looking at each other, done with the small talk, waiting for the other to speak.

"Quigley? I know this is probably not going to happen, but do you think I could have a hug? I could really use a hug."

I practically launched myself at him, and we stood there in the middle of the hall, hugging for what seemed like a wonderful eternity.

"I'm so sorry," he said, kissing the top of my head. "So, so sorry."

I felt like crawling into him, but settled for kissing his chest directly over his heart, wanting to somehow make all the pain go away. "No, I am. I know how it must have sounded that night. It wasn't like I really thought that stuff was no big deal. I know I kept saying things like that, but I didn't feel that way. I just wanted to protect Anne. I'm not good at half-truths. I got lost in trying not to let too much slip."

"I had no right to talk to you like that. It was just plain wrong. You can't imagine how ashamed I felt. I couldn't even face you enough to call. After I'd calmed down, I assumed you hated me and would never speak to me again."

"No, but I can see why you were frustrated. And I did stand back and not jump in when someone's safety was at stake. I totally get that. Even before I found out about what you went through and lost."

He shrugged. "I know it's a little obnoxiously chipper, but these days I try to think of it as what I went through and *found*. A new way. A new life. I mean, me? A jock?"

I giggled.

"Well, it's not that funny! But seriously, I was a different person then. You're going to think this is crazy, but after the accident, I was here at the hospital for a real long time. Months. Not fun. I had a roommate for a few weeks from California. We still talk when the occasional bad day gets us down. The guy was in a bad motorcycle accident out here, and they put us together while he healed enough to transfer home. His girlfriend was a model on a designer reality show shooting in L.A., so we watched a whole marathon of it. By the end, his girl had been tossed off when her designer lost one of the final challenges, and I was hooked. I could just see where the designers were missing that special something. Once I could get my good hand on fabric, it turned out that my brain could translate that to working with material, too."

"So that's why you can't draw! You're a leftie and you had to switch to right!"

He gave a sigh of exasperation, waggling a perfectly good left hand my way. "While I would like to blame my lack of talent on the accident, I'm just awful. Thanks for that, though."

We laughed and stood there holding hands in comfortable silence until I remembered his gift. "Oh! I got you something."

Zander pulled back the embossed paper and opened the portfolio.

"Happy birthday! I would sing, but you really don't want that," I said. "Might make these sick folks even worse."

"OMG, Quigley." He flipped through each page, reacting with a little gasp at several. "These are amazing. Truly."

I blushed and waved away the compliment. "I had good inspiration."

"It's all of my designs. You've found where they belong." He pulled me close and kissed me. "Thank you. This is the best present I've ever gotten. I love it."

"There's one more thing, but on the off chance you didn't hate me, I wanted to see if you wanted to go to the citywide show with me tomorrow and see it in person."

I pulled out the shot of the sketching couple. Zander stared at it for a long moment. "You're amazing."

I reveled in yet another snuggle. I could get used to this.

"So, you got the slot in the show!" he said, pulling back. "Excellent. I'm guessing Mr. Art King is not your biggest fan right now."

I thought of the "lonely goatherd" prank that could have cost me a scholarship, had I not blown it on my own. "Oh, it's mutual."

Zander laughed. "So what are you going to do with yourself today?"

"Wow, you know so much about my school now that you know when Senior Skip is?"

"Senior Skip?"

"It's an 'unofficial' official holiday for seniors. It always falls on the day of prom and all the seniors are expected to ditch. It started when all the girls were blowing off the last half of the day to get their hair and nails done."

"Ah. I'm afraid the seniors don't have the corner on the market today. Your whole school is closed. I saw it on the news while I was working out. I thought that's why you were here."

"Why is the school closed? Did they cancel prom, too?"

A shadow of hurt crossed Zander's face, covered quickly by a polite smile. "No, I guess you're still on for that."

"Not for me. Anne and I are having an anti-prom party at her house tonight. Lots of terrible-for-you frozen food, trashy celeb magazines, old John Hughes movies, that sort of thing."

"Sounds . . . fun?"

"*Yes*, fun. You just don't understand these things."

"But wasn't prom the whole reason you guys were working for Ms. Parisi this semester?"

"Sure. But it's okay, really. I got a one-hundred-dollar check for the regional essay contest, and added to the four hundred dollars I saved for the dress, it's exactly enough to buy myself an SLR digital camera. The kind that comes with different lenses that you can control F-stops on and adjust the way the picture is taken, like the old-school models."

"Sounds like you're decided."

"Yeah, I guess. Some things just aren't meant to be. Why is school closed, though?"

"Haven't you seen the news?"

My phone rang, earning a nasty look from the nurse.

"Those aren't allowed in here. They interfere with the medical machinery somehow," Zander said.

I nodded and tried to understand the jumble of words Anne blasted through the phone.

"I've got to go, Zander. Anne's freaking out about something. Do you think we could maybe talk tomorrow? Grab a coffee at ten before the show, or something?"

"Trying, but not thinking of anything that would make me happier."

I blew him a quick kiss as I was chased into the stairwell by the cell-phone-hating nurse.

· · · · · · · · · · · ·

Anne and I sat sharing a pint of Ben & Jerry's and surfing channels to catch more footage of Anne's baby sister. "You *could* just ask him for a video," I said. "They're new parents. They probably have a camera glued to that kid twenty-four/seven."

"I don't know. Seems kind of weird since I've never even met her yet. Did I tell you Dad lined up a gig doing a Broadway show next fall?"

"Only your dad could decide on a whim he wants to do Broadway."

"Hey, he's got an amazing voice. They've been after him for years to do a show. Getting Hollywood stars is their way of amping up the audiences—to find an actor who can actually sing is a bonus. He just wanted a chance to get to know me better and this at least brings him to the right coast. I think it's really sweet."

I hid my smile at the one-eighty a few weeks could bring. "I do, too."

"I still can't believe one of the guys 'fessed up to the cops," Anne said.

"I can't believe that they hid the light bar at school, backstage!"

"Well, that area is pretty impossible to reach. It's way above the stage curtain in the rafters. I just can't believe how many years of stolen traffic signs, statues, and highway patrol materials were stockpiled with it."

"I wonder if it was T-Shirt who confessed. If he was caught up in that group freshmen year, it could explain his dad's sudden generosity after hearing about Zander's accident and scholarship fund. Maybe there'd be no way to tie him to it specifically anymore, but a court might have gotten him even more," Anne mused.

"If the rest of the family is anything like Zander, I don't think they would be the type to sue. Maybe to put the guys away if they kept it up—to protect other people—but I can't imagine going after money just to get it. Zander seems to be in a pretty good place about what happened."

The doorbell chimed.

"Pizza!" We raced each other down the stairs.

Anne looked through the etched glass and whooped. "I think it's for you."

I took in her strange expression and uncontrollable giggles and opened the door as gingerly as one of those cans of nuts where fake snakes are about to pop out.

"Zander?"

He stood there, grinning. In a tux. Behind him waiting

alongside the mailbox was a long black limo. "Quigley, would you go to prom with me?"

I laughed. "Are you serious? I mean, yes! Or no—I don't have anything to wear."

He held up one arm and rustled the black garment bag laid across it. "Good thing I'm on pretty tight terms with an excellent designer." As he unzipped the bag, I recognized the flash of purple-and-red glowing material immediately.

"Zander! Yes, how did you—I mean—when?"

Anne grabbed me in a hug, jumping up and down.

"I just thought, prom being a once-in-a-lifetime experience, this might be one of those times you give this a *second measure before cutting*."

"You know about the speech."

"I do. Thank you. I can't tell you what it means to me. But hearing how you really get it, and weren't afraid to share, meant more than the money. So I decided a girl this special needs to be well taken care of." He gave a little bow and handed me the dress.

I giggled but glanced at Anne. "Can we take Anne with us?"

"Two lovely ladies on my arm, are you kidding? But wait, I might have a better option." He pulled out his cell, dialed, and held it out to Anne.

"Hello? Hi!" She playfully smacked Zander. "Yes. Well, yeah, I guess. Should we come pick you up?"

The rear door opened and out climbed The Spikester, sort of. A tamer version of The Spikester, with a few less metal accessories, carrying a garment bag of his own. Anne squealed and nearly bowled him over halfway up the walk jumping into his arms.

Halfway through their ten-minute welcome kiss, Anne broke away, "Oh, wait. I need to check in with my mom and make sure it's okay."

"It's okay." Ms. Parisi appeared like magic through the kitchen door bearing a camera. Shockingly, my parents were close behind. "Now go change so we can embarrass you by taking a million pictures like any proper parents would."

"I checked with Ms. Parisi and Quigley's folks before I ever arranged for the car," Zander said.

"My man Zander talked me up good." Lance nodded.

"Nothing but the truth," Zander said.

"Prom, school-sanctioned after-prom party at the bowling alley with faux gambling till dawn, watching sunrise at the waterfront, swapping cars before a late, greasy breakfast at the diner, and then off to Quigley's art show," Ms. Parisi ticked off the list. "While you kids are off, the Johnsons and I are going for our own evening out together. When chatting about logistics for tonight, your parents thought it was high time we got to know each other a little better, too!"

• • • • • • • • • • •

The hall looked more like a wedding than a prom, with white twinkly lights covering the walls and dripping like icicles down from the ceiling and chandeliers. A long aisle, surrounded by round candlelit tables with red rose centerpieces, led up to a dance floor in front of a stage. We posed for a group shot beneath the cheesy rose heart trellis backdrop and headed in to snag a table.

"Is it weird for you guys to be back in high school?" I asked Zander and The Spikester as I carefully adjusted the swirling silk of my skirt before sitting. Zander pulled his chair close behind mine and rested his chin on my shoulder with a sweet peck.

"Tough to notice your surroundings when you're blinded by beauty like this," The Spikester said as he twirled a giggling Anne and pulled her down onto his lap. He leaned toward Zander. "My God, we're incredible designers, aren't we? Oh, you girls look nice, too."

Anne playfully smacked his chest, earning her a deep, seconds-too-long kiss. Tonight, I didn't even mind.

"Nice, no. Breathtaking, yes," Zander corrected, sliding his fingers in mine and flipping my hand to gently kiss my palm.

"Awww. You guys clean up pretty well, too," I teased, embarrassed at the electric tingle Zander's lips left behind.

"Yeah, but I'm not so sure this tamed-down look really does it for me. You're not going soft on me, are you? How am I supposed to scandalize my mother when you look like this?" Anne asked as she pulled The Spikester's spike-free arms around her tighter.

"Oh, I've got plenty of scandal left in me, don't you worry." He nipped her neck. "Though I hate to break it to you, your mother likes me."

"Obviously, there's no future here, then," Anne called over one shoulder as The Spikester dragged her onto the pulsing beat of the dance floor. Anne shimmered in her faux wedding white with the jagged slit up one thigh.

An announcement with the number to text in the vote for prom king and queen momentarily interrupted the music.

"Do you guys mind that bringing us ruins your big shot at royalty?" Zander asked.

"God, no. That's hardly my thing, and Anne's not exactly

the traditional kind of girl, either. Besides, rumor is D. W. Bostwick, mathlete and computer nerd of the century, rigged the vote so that he and his date would win." I shrugged. "Who cares, anyway. I mean, do you even remember who the king and queen were at your prom?"

"I didn't go," Zander said softly.

I counted back the years, and my stomach dropped. "I'm sorry."

"Just didn't exactly feel important at the time."

"I guess not. Does it now?" An ache swelled in my chest as I thought of the things he'd missed out on that I took for granted. The music switched to a slow ballad that echoed the shift in mood.

"No. But being with you does."

I felt his breath on the back of my neck and heard the smile in his voice as he tugged on a lock of my hair. I turned, serious for a moment. "I'm here if you ever want to talk about it."

"I'd really, really like that. But not now." He jumped up and extended his hand with a smile. "Now, we dance."

We joined the slow swaying mass of bodies glued to each other on the dance floor. I leaned against Zander's chest and tried to memorize every touch and brush of his hand, inhaling the clean scent that made the rest of the world drift away.

"Bathroom," Anne commanded as the final notes of the song swelled.

Zander looked down and rolled his eyes with a fake exasperated sigh. "Okay, fine. Lance and I will just entertain ourselves by rating all these dresses passing by."

The Spikester nodded and leaned in, pointing a finger at a short figure walking away from us in an overly poofed version of Cinderella's ball gown with an exaggerated falsetto, "Hideouuuus!"

We followed Cinderella out and across the hall, into the bathroom. There was something familiar about her, but she slid into a stall before I caught her face.

"So, let me guess," I said from experience. "This is the moment when you explain you have to"—I raised my hands for air quotes—"stop for a bite to eat, and will catch up to me in a few hours."

Anne smiled at me from the far end of the mirror and stuck her tongue out. She leaned in to check her eyeliner. "I don't think so. Not this time."

"Really? Wow. Really, that's great—"

"Yeah, yeah. Don't make a big thing of it."

"Awww, my little girl's growing up," I teased her, dodging the blusher brush she threatened to throw.

The restroom's intercom interrupted the moment. "Announcing this year's king and queen of the prom . . . D. W. Bostwick and his date, Kallie Cristenson! Can we please have this year's royalty make your processional walk down the aisle to be crowned."

"Who the heck is Kallie Cristenson?" I asked.

"I am," said Cinderella smugly as she stepped out of the stall to wash her hands in the sink between us.

"Maria!" Anne and I both said at the same time.

Maria primped her updo and floofed out her disproportioned poofy cap sleeves. "Suckers," she spat at us and turned to me with a sneer. "Thought you could stop me from coming to prom by making David and T-Shirt afraid to show? Not only did I come, but I'm taking the crown. A freshman beating out all of those seniors! They'll be talking about this for the rest of my high school life."

"Even longer, I bet," said Anne from behind her in a mild voice, and smiled. "You really deserve this, Kallie."

Maria shot a superior glare over her shoulder before pushing past me. "Later, losers. I have to go get my crown."

Anne jumped forward to hold me back as we watched her flounce out of the bathroom, the back of her dress firmly tucked up into her stockings.

Chapter Nineteen

. . . .

We walked through the grassy lane between tents,
bleary-eyed from lack of sleep, but in excellent spirits.

"There's your division," said Anne.

The Spikester had to get home before his son woke up and
missed him, so it was just the three of us, strolling through
the park like it was the most natural thing in the world to
be wandering around in a tux and ball gowns at 9:45 in the
morning.

"Any sign of Foster Neuwirth?" Zander asked.

"Nope, but that looks like the pack of judges." I pointed
to a stern-faced group.

"They're not wolves, Quigley," Anne said.

I shot her a smile, but I wasn't so sure. They had a lot
of power traveling together like that. I assumed it would be
a secret-ballot arrangement, which somehow seemed more
comforting. This was like the real world.

I soon found out just how much like the real world this was.

"Wait. That's not mine." I pointed at a fairly decent photograph of a row of classic cars lit by a fading sun, with my school's name across it.

"What do you mean?" Anne asked.

"That's our slot, but that's not mine." I walked close enough to see the tiny crown in the corner. "David."

"You've got to be kidding me," Zander said.

The judges were just two easels away, jotting down notes and discussing in whispers. Zander walked up, waiting for them to finish.

"Excuse me. There's seems to be a problem with my friend's entry."

I held my breath as David approached the judges from the other side. He must have been lying in wait, like the snake he was.

"I don't think so. I'm sorry he's bothering you all," David butted in. "He doesn't even attend the school in question. I'm sure you all saw in the news about our little 'situation'? See, there's one of the girls involved." He pointed at Anne. "I'm sure you've seen the reports. Well, sadly, the original piece chosen for the show was damaged in all the chaos, so as the rules state, we defaulted to the runner-up."

"That doesn't even make sense! The gym where they found all of the stolen signs and the cop's light bar is on the other side of the school from the art studio!" I said. "He's lying. Where's my photograph?"

"I'm sorry, Quigley, as I said, it was damaged, so I went ahead and disposed of it for you."

At this, even the judges gasped. A petite woman with severely pulled-back hair eyed David shrewdly. "You disposed of someone else's artwork without asking?" The infamous gravely voice of Foster Neuwirth could bring anyone to his knees. David never stood a chance.

"Well, y-yes," he stammered. "There was water damage and I didn't want anything else being ruined. It was basically destroyed anyway." His voice had turned into a whine as streaks of desperation bled through.

"That's what he said about my entire classes' prints, including the negatives. Those he burned and then claimed I was smoking in the darkroom."

The judges grumbled. Art was sacred.

"Your piece is gone, Quigley. Get over it," David spat.

"Would you rather have nothing from our school shown?"

"Wait! Quigley made me a copy. I'll be right back." Zander sprinted toward the car.

The commotion attracted the notice of Mrs. Albertt, who had just arrived. The judges now looked so put out, I figured there was no hope—regardless, they wouldn't be judging anything attached to this nonsense without hating it.

Foster Neuwirth looked over David's print with a sniff of disdain. "And just what school are you planning to attend, young man?"

David puffed up. "Well, the Art Institute of Chicago or Michigan State; I'm not decided on which way to go yet."

"Well, you are now," said Neuwirth, and plucked the car print from the easel and dropped it into his hands. "*Go, Sparty.*"

Mrs. Albertt stepped forward. "If he's lucky. I think we'll have to have a little investigation into recent events on the campus before those final college reports head out. One of my colleagues pointed out that it appears we may have more of an issue with vandalism than we originally thought. I'm sorry for having doubted your word, Quigley. Consider your 'teacher's assistant' position reinstated."

Zander gasped for breath as he reached us, holding my print and his birthday portfolio. Foster placed the sketching couple on the easel and took a step back, saying something under her breath to the others that brought a relieved chuckle to the crowd.

"Passion, a unique technical touch. But the feeling overwhelms. I daresay, this is an emotion you've experienced." She raised her eyebrows, waiting for confirmation.

I glanced at Zander and blushed. Foster nodded with a knowing smile. "Though I don't know that old McCarthy would approve of the use of cameras in his gallery, this particular bench was always a favorite of mine."

She flipped open the portfolio, and her eyes widened the tiniest bit. She squinted down and then leaned back and gave me the once-over. "*Vogue* would love you for sketches and illustration," she murmured, and passed the portfolio to the others, holding the one featuring my prom dress up alongside me. "The designer?"

"Um, for the dress? The dress*es*? Zander," I pointed to my savior.

"*Vogue* would love you, too, young man," Foster said with a smile. "Ah, young love, full of talent—that will be an interesting story to watch. My ballot is cast in this battle, but the greater war is just beginning. What are your plans for further education, Miss Johnson?"

"Well, I had always thought I'd like to go to the Art Institute—"

"But she's still undecided, right, Miss Johnson? Taking that second measure?" A demure young woman with a kind smile stepped forward. "Mrs. Richards, Admissions, Rhode Island School of Design. I attended the banquet on Thursday. It is no surprise to see the passion, courage, and honesty expressed in your speech now reflected in your art."

Zander put his arm around my shoulder for a supportive squeeze. I decided this was a good thing in case my knees suddenly buckled.

"We don't like to lose our local talent. I'm prepared to offer you a full ride—room, board, and stipend—if you'd join us this fall. As I said, we were very impressed by your speech."

"I won?"

Anne grabbed my other arm and jumped up and down.

"I shouldn't talk out of turn, but yes . . . and no. The vote was unanimous. But when we referenced your written submission and realized an entirely different speech had been given, we had to award the prize to our second choice. Regulations. However, we at RISD appreciate nothing more than creativity. We'd love to add your out-of-the-box artistic spirit to our student population."

"Well, it certainly seems to be your day, Miss Johnson," Foster Neuwirth said. "I hope you realize the Art Institute would happily match any offer made by RISD. I see great potential, whichever path you follow. The choice is left to you, now."

I nodded, terrified for a moment, until the answer came from my heart. A sense of calm passed over me as I realized what I really wanted. "I can't say what this opportunity means, Ms. Neuwirth. But I think I've already found my perfect fit, right here at home."

Acknowledgments

Many thanks to George Nicholson, Regina Griffin, Erica Silverman, Alison S. Weiss, Mary Albi, and Nico Medina; to creative inspirations Nakoa Zuger, Janene Mascarella, Maggie and Don Ferris; to my dad for schlepping me to the Art Institute of Chicago with my sketch pad and charcoals; and my mom, who made every one of my prom dresses . . . and only sewed me in once.